THE PROFESSOR

Tshombe

T.S. AMEN PUBLISHING

Emeryville, California

For information, please send written queries to:
T.S. Amen Publishing
2340 Powell Street, PMB 110
Emeryville, CA 94608

ISBN:
978-0-9832001-5-4

Release Date: April 2015

DEDICATION

To the first professor, I dedicate this series and this book.
Plato.

Dear Students,

We each travel on our own individual path between birth and death. Today, each of your paths has intersected at these words. Think about that... These words have been written for you to find. Please pay attention to what has brought you these words. Imagine all the work, joy, and heartache that have gone into creating these pages. Consider all you've gone through just today in coming to this time and place. When you woke, a journey began and now this book is in your hands. How did we each arrive here? The Professor will answer this question for you. This book is an introduction to The World of Appearances: her/his story completed.

The Professor is a unique individual who discovered something about our existence. He wants to share this discovery with you. Ask yourself, how did we get here? Why? Where is our place in this vast universe? What is our role here on earth? Only the truth of humanity can adequately answer these questions for inquisitive minds. Prepare yourself for the future that awaits. Just as something has brought these words to each of us, something will move us past this experience and on to a new plane of consciousness. Please enjoy the experience of attending this prestigious class; we only accept the finest people in the world and you have been selected. The Professor is waiting to meet you.

Welcome to the class.

Sincerely,

Tshombe Amen

Chapter I: The First Class

I began this process by selecting a tested resistance. Only those who disobey the evil roles of man can withstand the process that follows. If you don't protest then you embrace ignorance and live in your master's knowledge, following instructions from a hidden unknown source.

"Good morning students, anyone who was not present for last week's orientation lecture please leave now. There will not be a review. Today ends your enrollment in this course. Everyone else, please wait; we will begin momentarily."

As I watched the herd of acceptors, I wondered how many of them actually knew what they were doing. How many of them really understood what I was doing? I told them to take the free ride -- the easy road. Follow my erroneous instruction. Some questioned why they had received the wrong start date for the class. I shook my head and continued waiting for all of them to leave. Only silence answered their uncertainty. They had received the correct date. The class starts now. Their minds are so easily defeated that accepting "no" is their only option. What they secretly desire is permission to be, instead of a demand to be. I'm sorry for those who left. The ones who stayed remained in disobedience because they wanted the truth. They demanded their justice by disobeying a command. They were the ones I wanted. Our spirits connected on the same path. Their voices were quiet. The herd was mumbling and gathering personal effects. Sounds we call speech gave their presence an echo of life. Language can be a beautiful stimulation for the body into ecstasy. The contrast is an ugly assault on our ego. Words are taught to us. Beliefs are intellectually stored. I am interested in the motives of those who stayed; they knew they were supposed to leave. The last of the herd galloped out. Now I could address these, the cunning survivalists truly at the top of the food chain.

"Thank you for your patience. Good hunters never rush to kill, and we all know this is the first day of class; you have taken a pop quiz of action and you have passed your first test. I see smiles. Yes, my young protestors, let us begin.

"How many of you can walk without assistance or any kind of support? Please raise your hands. Good. Good. Be thankful for motion without pain or struggle, there are many people who wish for motion without impairment. How many of you are thankful for your good health? Think about it... How many of you are consciously grateful for your health? Life can be much more difficult than it is now. You could be paralyzed. You could be missing a limb. You could be blind or deaf.

"This is a special class designed to facilitate a deeper understanding of human awareness. Most of you will think this is a psychological study, some will think this is a philosophical study, and many will not be able to define this class with a singular category. We will be examining questions such as: What are beliefs? What is the purpose of humanity? Why are we here?

"Now, I want you all to write these words as the heading in your notes: *I do not know anything.* I want you to read this statement. You can make it objective or subjective but this is all I will ask of you to write down. We know the things we learn, but what do we think about what we know? You can name all of the presidents, recite the laws of our country, you can diagnose all of the diseases on Earth, you can even find a way to balance the budgets of every country on Earth, but what do you *know* without the lessons of your experience? What have you learned that hasn't been taught to you? An impulse, you've been synthesized into an identity. You know math because...? You know language because...? The lawyer and the judge know law because it was taught to them. Doctors know medicine because it was taught to them. Is the doctor's experience with the rules of law more or less than the lawyer's in understanding the rules of medicine? We live like robots. Information drummed into our minds, our rooted instinct doing the rest. These are modern times from ancestors to descendants. Our thoughts piggy back off each other creating history: humanity is innovating evolution. Human creativity based on what we've learned through perception during exposure. Do you know the reason you exist? What do you know outside of your experiences?

Your choice to stay after being told the fallacy to leave is a desire to know beyond proclaimed authority's instruction. Our choices, our differences, dictate the impressions we leave and receive.

"Many go day-to-day performing rote rituals without acknowledging their place in the universe. We are orbiting a star at speeds greater than 65,000 miles per hour, yet we are worried about the trivial pursuits of bills, possessions -- the complexity of society. Living organisms have to be greater than eating, sleeping, and reproducing, right? Some believe in a divine presence. God, Allah, Jehovah, etcetera has placed us here to live a life of worship, and that those who oppose this divine decree should suffer the wrath of not honoring the higher power. Many follow these principles blindly through faith, implicitly trusting what they have learned through books and institutions. We are not here to challenge faith. The most powerful and motivating force in human existence is belief. Human beliefs have ruled the world for millennia. From small tribes, families and couples, to large cities, states, and entire countries, beliefs govern the day-to-day activity of all humans on Earth. We will not attempt to challenge beliefs, but we *will* attempt to gain a better understanding of them.

"As many have noticed there is no course outline for this class. The requirements are malleable. We will study each other. Our studies will be a reaction to and reflection of each other's thoughts, beliefs, and actions. Your thoughts will touch me as mine will touch yours. As I have stated, this is a groundbreaking course studying the areas where psychology, sociology, and philosophy converge. Each of you has been referred to this course by a select group of staff. Your work in previous classes means nothing. Your psychological profiles have been disregarded. *You are here for a reason.* Twelve of you sit before me, but only five will be selected to study this course. Those selected will receive five credits toward their major, fulfilling a requirement of their choice. This is a great incentive. Still, you must pass this course in order to receive your credit. To pass this course you must receive an A. You must commit to excellence to succeed. You are pioneers, the first students of this course. You will set a precedent, creating the foundation for how this course will be studied.

"For two hours Monday, Tuesday, Wednesday, and Thursday we will be together. If you are one of the chosen and you miss a class, do not bother coming back; perfect attendance is required. Your first assignment is to write on the topic of life, specifically why life is important to you. This assignment is due today. No assignments will be accepted after five o'clock. Drop your assignment through the slot on my office door. Ladies and gentlemen, this has been today's class."

As I gathered my belongings, I could hear the whispers begin among the students. It was ten-thirty in the morning. All stayed knowing they were supposed to leave. Over forty-five students enrolled in this class. Twelve stayed. I owed the Dean a hundred dollars. I just knew more than fifteen would resist.

I sat in my office thinking about this place called earth, a water planet where human life studies everything around the perspective of our limited linear perception. Many of us don't truly observe the big picture staring at us since the dawn of existence, yet all of our experiences have been in the presence of this truth. A truth for everything on this planet. We've all stood, lay, or crawled under the sky, the stars, moon, and comets. Every human who's ever lived has shared the experience of being, but how many of us consider the connection we share? For thousands upon thousands of years, some tight knit groups have been thinking about it. The human masses pushed in a predetermined direction through injections and innovations; their minds controlled by someone else's creations. The students' answers would tell me which of them is... willing.

Why is life important to you? The first response slid through the slot in the door.

Student one: *Life brings me forward deeper into love. My eyes close tightly as I breathe. The light shines upon me. I am free. I am everything intertwined with harmony. I love my life.*

As I contemplated those words more answers came through the door. *Why is life important?*

Student two: *God gave us life and the life God gave us is sacred.*

10

Student three: *As a child wondering in the darkness, I never knew light. When I saw it, I was afraid. Now I see I shouldn't be, and still, I don't see life's importance. Still here being me.*

Student four: *Does life represent me? What is life? I want to know.*

Student five: *Life is the reason I exist. The existence of my life is to exist. I am in a state of formed opinions and beliefs called my ego, my identity.*

More papers fell through the door.

Student six: *The breath in my body is sacred. I am here to pass on this breath as this breath was passed on to me.*

Student seven: *A precious gift, my existence. I am who I am and who I am is the reason why I even experience this. Look at me.*

Arrogant fool number seven. I balled up the seventh assignment and threw it in the trash. A sweet fragrance filled my nostrils as the sharp staccato of a woman's high heels approached. Instead of one, two answers. My mind was left wondering which answer came from the scent so sweet I could taste it. The sound of the heels faded. The fragrance lingered.

Student eight: *How can I list the ways my life is important to me? There is no particular reason life is important to me. God gave me life. My family… My life. There is so much to be thankful for. Here we are. I enjoy it. Meditate, pray, or take medication.*

Student nine: *Life is not that important. Events, occasions, are moments in life leaving nothing more. What we think is not life. Everybody dies. What's so important about that?*

The puzzle was easy to solve; I knew which answer was from the sweet smelling heels.

Student 10: *The truth, the lie, the reality, the illusion all we know. In our confusion of being, we search for the purpose of existence. We continue life as important to be.*

Time marched on in silence; three-hours passed before another answer came through the door. I counted every second of those three hours, each minute an eternity. In an attempt to feed my curiosity, I reviewed the answers in my possession. I read each line over and over, studying the patterns of their writing: Did they write on a hard surface or soft surface? Was their penmanship rushed or did they take their time while writing their answers? It was all I could do to keep from looking at the slot in the door or the spot on the ground where the paper would fall. I heard footsteps outside and wondered if they were for me. A potential student? My heartbeat quickened; my palms and brow perspired; I refused to breathe until the footsteps outside passed my door. My heart sunk as the steps faded. I resumed my wait to hear footsteps meant for me.

Student 11: *My ID number 420-12-0392. DOB: 11/19/92. Why am I more than this? I am what has been taught to me. I am what they want me to be. A number and a name.*

My last true day of naïveté was the date of this student's birth. My last supper was their first breath. The heartbeat, the mind of that date, here with me in living form. The answer created for me.

No more came to the door.

Chapter II: The Second Class

The next morning I watched the changing faces of twelve students as they filed into the room, wondering who amongst them had been chosen. Today, we would share fate.

"Students, good morning. I have received your assignments and I have made my selections. There are twelve people in this room. Most of you will be excused from this class. One of you shouldn't have come at all. Let us begin.

"Debora Emch, please step forward. You have been selected for this class."

Ms. Emch was answer number nine: *Everybody has to die. What's so important about life?* I gestured for her to sit in one of the five chairs behind me. She sat in the chair furthest to my left.

"Traci Thick, please step forward. You have been selected for this class."

She was answer number four: *What is life?* A direct request. I felt her need to know. I gestured for her to sit in one of the chairs behind me; she chose the chair furthest to my right.

"Daniel LaDay, please step forward. You have been selected for this class."

Mr. LaDay was answer number five: *I am important and so life is important to me.* He will know his true importance. He had the right answer. He stepped forward, smiling, looking back at the other students. I gestured for him to have a seat in one of the three remaining chairs behind me. He sat next to Ms. Emch as I called another student.

"Wesley Macpherson! You have been selected for this class."

He was answer number three: *Wondering in the dark and being afraid of the light.* He was the essence of the journey; he was a student of this class before he met me. Mr. Macpherson took his time slowly moving to one of the two remaining seats behind me. He sat next to Ms. Thick.

"The final student accepted to this class is Geraldine Amen."

Ms. Amen was answer 11, the answer created for me. She took the remaining seat in the center. This small woman's presence gave me chills. She moved like fire in the flesh. November 19, 1992 now sat behind me in the center chair. *Why is life important?*

I turned to address the seven remaining people in the room.

"Of those who remain, six of you were not chosen. One of you is here for an unknown reason. I received eleven papers. I've chosen these students from the eleven, yet there are seven of you remaining. Why are you here? You didn't turn in your assignment, yet you report to class anyway? Is it to explain why you couldn't perform your first assigned task? Am I supposed to forgive you and allow you to make it up? This is real life ladies and gentlemen. You cannot undo what you've already done. If you are late for your train or your bus to work, the train or the bus is gone. Those of you who are resourceful will find a way to get to your destination. For others this will result in a detour from the course you've chosen. You represent the percentage of people who miss out. You are a factor in the statement, 'wrong place, wrong time.' You are, in this moment, in the wrong place at the wrong time. The class has been selected. If you are not sitting behind me, you are dismissed. No questions. Please leave now."

I studied the eyes of each person exiting the lecture hall. All but one met my gaze; she took the longest to leave. Curly locks of greasy dark hair obscured her face. She shook hands with everyone in the room; she was connected to something here, I could feel it.

The class was now clear of outsiders. I walked around to make sure all entrances and exits were secured before I addressed the students. I listened as they made casual conversation. I wanted to see who was connecting with whom. Mr. Macpherson was being bombarded with questions from Ms. Thick, who appeared to be conversing with herself. Mr. Macpherson shrugged his shoulders to acknowledge his presence in the conversation. Mr. LaDay, on the other hand, was speaking to Ms. Emch in a manner of conquest rather than one of peer interaction. I overheard him say something to the effect of, *a pretty girl like you shouldn't be in a place like this*. You look like you should be in movies. She smirked at the insult. Ms. Amen

14

watched me with an unbroken gaze. Even as the other students tempted her with conversation, her fixated eyes never shifted from my place in the light. My vision met hers; she persisted until the power of her gaze made me turn away. Her stare burned into me as I addressed the room.

"Class! Here we are, this is our group. I'm here, as are you, to learn. All are teachers, all are educators. We all have observations to share. Consider me as you consider yourself, a student. We are peers.

"The first order of business will be one-on-one interviews with me in my office. You are to decide the order in which each of you will be seen. I will be awaiting your decision at my desk."

I walked away hearing the hushed discussion begin. At my desk I sat wondering if they would form a hierarchy or maybe introduce a democratic equality by voting. Ms. Emch came in first.

She moved with reservation. Her arms folded as if holding herself to keep warm. Her eyes scanned for pertinent details as she walked into my office. This beautiful woman had no idea what to expect. I was curious to find out why she was chosen first; they'd made their selection quickly. She was certainly not the most dominant member of the group. The ice-breaker: she told me the students' method of selection. They placed numbers one through five in a hat. She picked number one. I found the random number selection a delightfully unexpected method.

I asked Ms. Emch a series of questions. Her responses gave me the following: In her thirties she enrolled in college as a promise to her daughter whom she conceived at eighteen. Her daughter's father died before the child was born. She'd married since, but was recently divorced. Her goal is to be a developmental psychologist. She wants to help people with complex issues. My summation: the lifestyle she lived while growing up: drinking, drugs and casual sex, led to more troubling choices until this point in her life. I felt a sense of urgency in Ms. Emch's story. She was searching for a pleasure worthy of her life's devotion. She wanted to be free from the emotional, unbalanced cycle of fear. Her ex-husband abused her physically and mentally. Her mannerisms pointed to her having been abused in other relationships

15

as well. She looked to other people for answers in vain, only finding pain, sorrow, anger, and frustration. The evil demons of feelings that hurt the soul. This journey back to school was a search for something she lost. The lost child of life dwelling in her spirit. The adult reflection formed in a cast of molded by impressions from experience. It was a promise to her daughter. Her return to school another external search for internal clues; an assignment she accepted from another outsider, her child. Ms. Emch. She would learn that all answers come from the observation of perspectives. I thanked her for her time. I looked forward to seeing her in class.

No longer than a minute passed before Mr. LaDay walked through the door. A strikingly handsome African-American man, his demeanor exuded confidence. He was one of my younger students, only two years out of high school. He came from a wealthy family and had entered college for the same reasons as most kids his age: his family's encouragement and socially driven aspirations propelled him to where he stood today. His goal was to become a doctor in the field of psychiatrics. My summary of him after the interview: If left to his own choices without the pressures of society or family, he would most likely not be in college. He enjoyed the Viking pleasures of life: women, drink, and competition. He felt a need to outdo those around him. His goal of becoming a psychiatrist was an extension of his personality. Exploring the problematic differences in individuals was merely his way of justifying his pursuit of pleasure and competition. He defined himself by understanding the joy and misery of others. Soon he would find the true meaning of the happiness he seeks. He would gain a new perspective into the world around his form. I thanked him for his time and asked for the next student.

Ms. Thick radiated beauty. Her style, fashion, and presence spoke volumes. She reminded me of an advertiser's imagination directed toward perfect beauty. I could imagine men and women alike projecting all sorts of fantasies upon her. My summary of her after the interview was that she's often been treated like a celebrity upon initial meeting, and then she speaks and all the mental images of what a celebrity should be are slowly wiped away by her insecurities. Her

16

incessant rambling, born from a fear of silence, destroys all question and curiosity about what she thinks or who she is as a person. She will tell you anything you want to know and things you never asked for. She is a woman in her late twenties who comes from a middle-class family and works part-time for spending money. Her parents provide what they can. Unlike the rest of the students, Ms. Thick seems to have no direction. When asked about her aspirations she stated she wants to be an actress, though without formal training or any experience. She is attending college to work toward a science degree in case her acting career doesn't work out, but has no particular science field in mind. Her facade projects the illusion she has dreamed up, but in reality, Ms. Thick does not believe in her own capabilities. She wants others to believe in her aspirations, while she exists in the moment, living contrary to momentary choices that lead to future manifestations. Dreams without work are lies to the spirit. Sprits reflect our truths and gnaw at the lies we want reflected in our outside appearances. Pain suffocates her self-confidence. She is not worthy for what she imagines. She blocks doubt with imagination. Her deep desire to know the truth for happiness is the sole reason I accepted her.

Ms. Thick was answer number four. I knew who she was when she dropped off her paper. Her desire to know far exceeds the others'. She epitomizes the lie society forces us to accept, and I believe we will all learn a lot from her. The eyes of fame lie to celebrities about who they are. An intelligent woman who denies her own brilliance will learn truths about reflection cannot be found in the false images that others project for her. Happiness is not found in a department store. Joy is not found on a movie screen. Understanding is not found in the pages of celebrity gossip columns. I thank Ms. Thick for her time and ask her to send in the next student.

Mr. Macpherson looks the part of a star quarterback. His 6'2" frame and muscular build establish a powerful presence. He didn't smile much and looked as if he'd rather be somewhere else. He seemed to be on a clock of some type. As with the others, I ask Mr. Macpherson the same series of questions to gain insight into how he sees himself. His one or two word answers caused our conversation to resemble an interrogation rather than an interview. As he grew more comfortable with being late on his agendas, he revealed why he was enrolled in college. He loved his sport and his coach encouraged his education. He did not mention family. He expressed his interest then he said that whatever he does in college will be for his community. Our interview was interrupted by a text from his coach. The stopwatch. He was late for practice. I would have to rely on my review of his file to fill in the blanks about his background. Orphaned, his early life was spent in foster care. He entered when he was six years old. His mother overdosed on narcotics. His father was not named on his birth certificate. His life represented a symptom of the illusions against the reflected being: the world of humanity lost in a misguided struggle for purpose. In society's process of searching for purpose, the misguided and misunderstood inflict the energy of their pain and frustration onto our collective being and that energy manifests in the form of human existence: Mr. Macpherson was here to find his truth of being. I thanked him for his time and asked to see the final student.

I waited an oddly prolonged time. I went to the door and walked out into the lecture hall. No one was there. I called out her name,

"Ms. Amen?"

No one answered. I went back into my office and found her sitting in my chair extending a piece of paper toward me. She smiled. I ask how she got in my office. She gestured for me to take the paper from her hand. It read, *I am deaf and I do not speak. I do not sign in the conventional manner. I read lips, body language, and gestures. Accept me. Please.*

Chapter III: The First Students

More than fifty revolutions around the sun and my experience in the world of human existence has reached an apex. I feel as if there is little left for me to enjoy in unforeseen phenomena. The majority of humans and other living things struggle in bodies born dying, under the attack from other dying bodies hungry to survive. Who knows the Truth of ancient secrets from a governing covenant that isn't locked away, cast out, or so afraid to speak that they forget the sound of their own voices? Who keeps their knowledge restricted to a small circle in order to retain power and control over ignorance? Kings, queens, dictators. Truth unwittingly becomes trapped in the retention of power, unable to break from its desperate grasp. With nowhere, no real place other than fantasy to run to and escape from their fear based creation, our only choice is to accept the walls of protection created to keep us in the city's street-maze of ignorant confusion. I am forced to accept the ignorance of the masses in an ambivalent harmony which tests the limits of my sanity on a daily basis. I am plagued by understanding. My only recourse is this class, sharing a purpose known only to a chosen few.

In my attempt to flee, I stumbled upon the life I lead today. Many years ago I was someone else. My name was different. My face was different. My view of the world was shared with a scant selection, while the many lived in blissful ignorance. A career-driven bio-physicist with ideas of changing the world, I pledged my life to becoming a pioneer in my field. With perfect SAT scores, PhD's from two of the top schools in the world, I.Q. scores off the charts, and the work ethic of a honey bee, I was poised to become one of the greatest physicists in history. I soared to the top of my field; within five years of graduating college, I was working in one of the top research laboratories in the country. The lab worked on groundbreaking bioengineering and astrophysics concepts. I obtained top-secret government clearance within two years. My blissful ignorance stood poised to be shattered. There are some things humanity shouldn't know.

A person driving through my old community would see normality at its finest: children playing, homes for sale, bustling shops, and people going about their seemingly normal activities. We lived in a military owned subdivision. Only top personnel with special clearance were truly aware of what went on inside the laboratory. As a scientist with the highest levels of education the world offered, I couldn't morally grasp the things we were doing – we were cloning human beings. When I received my clearance they told me if I divulged the works of the company to anyone, the company would find out and the punishment would make me crave the mercy of death. They showed me videos of men and women locked in underground bunkers forced to work. They told me they didn't like doing this to workers because it didn't promote good production. They found those who believed in our quest would work harder for the good of the country. I chose to become one of those who worked for the good. I believed in the Truth. I understood its meaning and I was honored to be part of such a beautiful secret. I understood who we are, what we are. Books made for laymen or "normal", as I call them, do not cover this work. Information as wild as imagination can conjure, virtually impossible for any normal to understand. A Truth that would shatter all they believed, all they think they know.

To challenge human beliefs is the most dangerous thing any person can do. I carried a secret and worked hard to do everything they directed me to. The more I worked the more I learned. Each new thing more troubling than the last, until the day I learned their true intentions. It shook me. I became uneasy around them and they noticed. They noticed the change in my behavior. I tried to leave. They followed me. Out of fear I returned, hoping they hadn't caught on. It didn't work; they were on to me. I told them I'd left because I needed a break, a vacation. They seemed to accept my explanation and on the basis of my intelligence and my work they seemed to overlook my attempted escape. It was a ruse. I didn't think for one second I'd fooled them. They had seen this before. They knew. They knew what I was thinking before I did. Human behavior is easily patterned. I was headed to an underground lab, unless I made my escape. I would have to give up all I had ever known.

I bathed in ice water until my body temperature reached dangerous levels of hypothermic shock. With a lead blanket and all of the cash in my possession I made my escape. Almost instantly my face was plastered across the nation as a murderer. The next day everyone who saw the broadcast was looking for me. Dressed as a woman, I lived on the streets, my life in complete disarray. I weighed suicide against a life in prison. My solution found me in the form of a blind man named Carl. From the first time he spoke to me he was my friend.

"How long do you think it will be before they find you? I'm sure you realize this way of living cannot go on very long. "

A blind man stood in front of me and knew my identity upon first contact. Without as much as a hello he offered me advice. Was he one of them? Was he sent to capture me? The people who protect the Secret are everywhere and I had the power to expose their truth; paranoia at its finest. My logical mind told me to flee. My natural instincts told me to stay. I slowed my mind to focus my thoughts. If Carl wanted to harm me he didn't need to warn me by telling me he knew who I was. He continued,

"They will find you unless you get help."

From that moment, we were connected.

I accepted his offer of assistance and he introduced me to a network of friends who could help. I'm not sure how many of them fully knew the depth of our situation. I never spoke of plans with anyone other than Carl. My new friends were supporters with their own ideals and beliefs about the system, advocates and protesters who, from their positions of oppression, wanted to stop the greed and corruption of our world leaders. They asked no questions about my situation, offering only suggestions and solutions to the matters at hand. A doctor changed my face. A few papers changed my identity. This secret changed my life.

Just like me, Carl, now my dearest friend, was chased from civilized society. Once an agent for the Company, he described his role in the Truth as the perfect split between fantasy and reality. He and the other agents stood on this divide protecting the Secret from society, and society from itself. Like my former self, he believed in the good of what we were doing. He believed what they told us to believe until he accidentally discovered our real purpose. This discovery cost him his sight and his life as he knew it.

Like a leper banished from his village, he wandered the streets blind in search of a place to call his own, haunted by the last image he ever saw. He expressed the pain and confusion he suffered at the hands of his own masters. He had devoted his life to serving them. He opened a door one second too early and for that mistake his life would never be the same. They took his sight, bagged him up like trash, and threw him from a moving vehicle into an unknown abyss. He was a man who had never existed. A man who carried a Truth no one wished to hear. Unlike me, he was not pursued; he was banished. Unable to rise from the ashes, he found comfort in the streets to which he'd been abandoned.

The normal world would not understand him. He would not commit to the performance necessary to exist in harmony with society. An actor, forced to lie and never able to speak of the Truth. He found comfort in the world of homelessness. There, people did not judge him; they accepted him for who he was: a homeless, blind man. He could speak the truth without fear; no one would care about his rants of aliens and secret societies. He created a community of supporters using his brief glimpse of the Truth as his guide. Carl didn't know the full Truth until I told him. He only knew what he had seen and what he had pieced together from that one experience.

One day when we'd gotten closer, I asked Carl how he knew who I was when we crossed paths. How did he know I wasn't guilty of the things I'd been accused? He said there were two red flags that led him to believe something was different than what the media spoke. When the news broke my education was revealed; the science background piqued his interest. Then, the people who were looking for me were from the Company. He'd put out many false stories and he knew agents when he saw them. They only looked for special people. That's how he knew I had not done what the media said I did. He waited and watched me through the eyes of others while he protected me from the Company. When he was sure about me he made his move. My friend.

After my surgery, through his network of friends, Carl found a safe place for me where I could recover: a secluded room behind a dry cleaner's with a back alley entrance. A filthy, roach infested, chemical scented room was a palace compared to the places I'd lived since my escape. Carl visited me almost every day during my recovery. Most times, we'd sit and talk about the future of humanity, about a world without the Truth's protectors or about the endless possibilities of existence in observation. As I healed, Carl guided me to my new way of life. In exchange, Carl only wanted one thing. He asked me this question when I was ready to leave: "Can you promise me you'll expose the Truth of human existence to those willing to know?" He left me without an answer.

I twisted in turmoil for many days wrestling with what fulfilling this promise would mean for my life. After all I'd done to hide from them I did not want to face them again. I wanted to go back to the blissful ignorance that was my life before science during college, or even high school when everything was idealistic. I wanted to disappear among the vast moving crowds of daily life and forget all that I had seen in my previous days. It was possible. With time and effort I could possibly block out my old life. I could start a new family. Children. Home. Love. The joys of life. How could I deny myself those things to fulfill a promise? How could I refuse the man who'd rescued me? Could I even live up to this promise? Deny the world a Truth which could set humanity free? His request would be difficult to fulfill and it could cost me my life to fulfill it. Countless people before me have tried to reveal it to the masses, only to be destroyed by its reality. How could I sacrifice myself for something so impossible to do?

I entered my fourth day of contemplation when a revelation came during an afternoon journey downtown. I traveled from my humble dwellings into the abyss of humanity. The seas of the flowing masses traveling to and fro swallowed me completely. I fit myself into the movement. I flowed in whatever direction I wished, carried by the command of my own will with no particular place to go. I stopped. I stopped moving in the midst of a downtown street on a weekday afternoon. The masses moved around me. Some bumped into me. Others stared at me as though I was an oddity of nature. The bandages on my face, noticed by those around me, seemed to take on meaning. The strangers' expressions upon seeing me made their faces appear as twisted as mine. An older woman with a weathered face and wisdom in her eyes stopped.

"Are you in need of help?"

"I'm fine." I replied.

She said, "Some people search all of their lives for wishes instead of being thankful for the life that grants them existence." She gripped my hand tightly, "Always be thankful for the things you have."

She let go of my hand and said no more words. Within moments she was absorbed back into the ocean of human masses. I stood there surrounded by the rivers of people absorbing what she'd said to me. I knew what I had to do. I took a deep breath and moved into the traffic of human existence. People moved back and forth with all sorts of ideals, beliefs, and opinions. I stood among them with a gift so precious and so pure it could solve all our problems in one fell swoop. I decided to make the promise. In that moment I chose to devote my life to sharing my gift with the world; a gift I was thankful to have.

People see me now, in my daily profession, at face value. My role as an educator is to pass my knowledge to those who are worthy of understanding its meaning. I grasp my sense of purpose from my promise.

Carl never returned to my humble dwelling behind the dry cleaner's. When I was healed and eager to enter the world, I went outside for fresh air and found a small boy standing at my door. He handed me a letter addressed to *Professor*; he said it was from Carl. I looked away for only a moment as I opened the letter and the boy vanished as if he was never there. The letter might as well have fallen from the sky. I couldn't help but wonder if there had even been a boy at all – he looked like me at that age.

I went back inside with the message from Carl. I sat on the couch and prepared myself for whatever the mysterious envelope contained. *Professor?* Hmm... I opened the letter and found three items: a birth certificate, a letter, and a key. My heart beat furiously and the pace of my breath quickened as I felt my duty.

Dear Friend,

We all face challenges in life which shape our perception of the world. Some view change as adversity while others embrace it as a way of life. The world is full of people who are afraid of change. No matter how much they chant in the favor of change, no one wants drastic change. No one desires to alter all they have ever known to be true. The type of change brought by wars on your homeland, the type of change brought by invasion, we resist.

You have accepted my offer and your promise is not to me more than it is to yourself and the rest of the world. Your promise will find you when you forget yourself. Your promise will understand you when you are misunderstood. Your promise will push you forward when you no longer have the will to move. Everything is for a reason. Everything is for the best. The will that has brought you to the place you find yourself today is divine. You have been chosen. You are the one who is to reveal the truth. It is your destiny, your path.

As you embark on your journey, know you will face resistance. People will fight the gift of change. People who aren't supposed to hear this Truth will wish to do you harm, my friend.

I have prepared a path for you to express this Truth. Below is an address. Go to this place and instructions will find you. As for the key, my friend, always keep it close. You will know what it's for when the time comes. I sincerely thank you. Fight strange lies with the resistance of belief. Do not fault them for their ignorance. Choose your disciples well. Be aware of the Protectors. Be aware of the non-believers. I will always be near. Whenever you need me, I will be close. Be safe, my friend. You are the Professor of Truth. We are One with you. We are One with all.

Your friend,

My new life began. The surgery to change my appearance only secured my safety from those who wished to do me harm. The help Carl provided was a relief, but that did not give my new life meaning. Even my promise to Carl did not give me meaning. It was not until I received this letter that I understood the purpose of the life I now lead as the Professor.

The address on the letter led me to an affluent part of the city. After months of living in squalor, the pleasing sight of upscale shops, clean streets, and an elevated standard of living relieved me. This is the environment I had been used to before my persecution. My recent way of life was anything but glamorous. Draped in clothing donated to the church, a button-up shirt and some slacks that had seen better days, I arrived at the address on the letter. It was a beautiful building rich in historical details. The doorman greeted me with a smile. I could smell the wood and plaster, decades older than myself. I felt a sense of comfort. This location provided in Carl's package; it was safe. I gave the doorman the suite number from my letter along with the name: Dr. Washington. The doorman asked my name. I was startled; for a minute I didn't know what to say.

The words passed my lips as though I never said them, "The Professor."

The doorman smiled.

"We've been expecting you."

Dr. Washington's home exuded wisdom and comfort. He was a collector of fine art. His home spoke volumes about who he was. I took an educated guess that he was a man of distinguished character. Having traveled the world and studied abroad, he was a well-rounded man with an extensive library. The lack of clutter denoted an orderly man who understood everything has its place.

He stood before me, rather diminutive in stature, with a gesture to have a seat in a well-worn, overstuffed chair behind me. He put his hands behind his back as I took my seat in the chair. In front of me he began to pace the Persian rug.

"I am the Dean of admissions at a very prominent University. I have doctorate degrees in behavioral psychology and sociology. I have studied in Europe, Africa, South America, and Asia. I've always questioned human purpose and scientific origin. Where did all of this begin? How did we go from cave and valley dwellers to chemists and astronauts? What is the universe? Why is human life so complex? Is there a higher purpose for this life? Is the answer in sacred texts? These questions plagued my mind to no end. Then, there were answers, a Truth that answered all my questions. I no longer wonder why. I now wonder how. How did we let this happen? How do we change this? I met Carl while volunteering at the local clinic doing psychiatric evaluations. Through many conversations, he and I developed a friendship and camaraderie based on our shared beliefs. Professor, I base my conclusions on logical reasoning. With analysis as my foundation and skepticism as my framework, my conversations with Carl led me to believe he was no ordinary blind person roaming the streets of our city. His I.Q. score higher than my own and his travels of the world more extensive. He, by all accounts of studies, facts, statistics, and percentages should not be a homeless man. I offered him my assistance, he shared with me the cause of his enlightenment. That is what has brought us here today. My journey has led me from curiosity to understanding, and I believe sharing this understanding will help heal our world.

"Carl informed me of your mission during our last visit. He requested my assistance in helping you to fulfill it. I'm not sure how we're going to accomplish this feat. Through my talks with Carl, I have an understanding of what it is you wish to do. As I said before, my curiosity and intellect have led me here today. I am aware of certain questionable practices in our society. I've always analyzed and deduced information around me. Face value has rarely been my take on a given situation. I do have a propensity to over-analyze. I believe it is safer to over-analyze than to be misguided by ignorance. This situation is not the result of excessive analysis. I believe there is something more to our existence than simply existing. That's why you're here. My dear Professor, I've been informed by the Collective you hold the key to the final, haunting questions. I am here not only to help you, but to serve as your assistant and become a disciple of your teachings."

A chill swept across my flesh reaching into my bones, seeping into my beating heart. To have a man with his level of dedicated study sit before me seeking the wisdom to understand his own purpose instilled in me the necessary proof that I'd made the right decision to live this mission of existence. Here was a man who studied at the finest universities, a man who had touched most of the continents on Earth, sitting before me seeking my assistance in understanding himself. In that moment, I felt the passion of what I was here to do: my promise, my purpose. The power of it surged through my body. My spirit alive. The Professor of Truth born to teach in a world of lies.

Meeting Dr. Washington was the highlight as my first day being the Professor. We understood the Truth belongs to everyone and it was our duty to show humanity this purpose. Finding those who seek harmony without a desire to judge or define being with the ability to see all life forms as the key to unlocking creation's purpose. We developed a special class at the University where we could cultivate the Truth; tilling the fertile soil of young minds thirsty for knowledge. Whatever their missions in life, the studies here would guide them

To keep our teachings clandestine the students have to be kept ignorant of the true subject in their studies. They will earn the proof of tested discoveries; dressed up in social standards; no radical red flags to provoke resistance, the new, smaller, almost private course to the University would garner very little notice. Dr. Washington got the class approved as an advanced lab, open study course for students who maintained a 3.9 grade point average or higher. Credits earned through our class would then be applicable to their majors. Instead of advertising for students we looked through their academic profiles to select them. We narrowed the number of students even further by separating those willing to disobey an instruction we knew to be incorrect. Out of fifty students we'd select five.

I was brought to the University with a background bestowed upon me compliments of the Underground. They had thought of everything.

28

My face, my job, my life, was in the image of a man who quietly disappeared a few months earlier during a working vacation to an African jungle; no one reported him missing. He was a man with an illustrious career who redefined mental incapacity from a legal perspective. He was a professor of psychology and sociology. He wrote a premier book about sociology and conducted psychological experiments on criminally insane patients, from which he proved 90% of them were fit to stand trial, despite their mentally ill diagnoses. His experiment became a precedent for law. A wave of mentally ill patients flooded the American prison system over the next two decades using his revised standard of assessment. Instead of expensive hospitals providing care at the cost of taxpayers, inexpensive prison healthcare covered the cost of the mentally ill housing and treatments. Powerful hospital insurance companies invested fortunes to combat the diagnosis designed by my new persona. Much was at stake, and now, without any notice, he'd been replaced by me.

The financial freedom I inherited from the original professor was an immense reward. I lived a life of quiet extravagance with money as no worry from book sales, speaking engagements, lectures, book signings, and tours, in addition to being the highest paid professor at the University. I ate the best foods. I slept on the finest sheets and found my every desire at my fingertips. A man of greatness in this microcosm. I was back, alive, and free reign was mine. I studied every inch of this life with my first student, the Dean, at my side. After a wonderful summer of designing, planning and structuring, we were given the green light to start the class.

Chapter IV: Mental Illness

"'*Fire!*' I scream as I burn, but no one comes to help me. My eyelids, long since vanished to incineration. Eyes dry, no moisture for my vision. Forced to watch myself in reflection as I burn. No tears for my cry. The anguish from my burning flesh consumes me. My spirit loses its connection to flames that sear pieces of my body. Again I scream, '*Fire!*' and no one comes to witness my ego losing its identity of self.

"I was born in a place built of water. Breath comes through the wind. My first taste of fresh air forges the connection of spirit and body. My energy feeds off bodies void of spirit. A piece of energy captured in limited existence, life until death. The whole of the individual is an individual part of the whole. Without body energy returns to the essence of creation. Freed from the ego of reflection, unification with all captures and absorbs me back into the author of life's constitution. I am in everything, and everything is within me.

"As I burn I scream, '*Fire!*' No one comes to help me. I'm losing my connection with being. I sleep. One with all seeks to understand the space being in my form.

"I rise from the ashes of substance still hearing the echoes and gurgles of my past screams. Happily I leave this form. To escape the pain of missing pleasure. Formlessness lives inside a constant, eternal orgasmic pleasure. No! No! Devilish arms pull me back. My body. I feel numbed nerves connecting in the breath of spirit. Why? The voice connected to the arms pierces through air-filled ears. I'm trapped again."

"Vida! Vida! You have not been burned. You are alive. You are not dead. Vida! Do you hear me? Vida! Can you hear me? Vida! It's me! Dr. Muerte, your doctor. Do you recognize me?"

"I tell the voice who calls my name that we live the life of unlimited realities. All other Beasts live the limited reality of their physical possibilities. We live in unlimited moments of invention created by the spirit's dreams and nightmares born of ego's experience. We exchange energy with all we touch: the temptation to leave behind a reflection of identity directs our moments toward exhausting creation's quest for exploring the experience of all realities. *Why doesn't anyone hear me?!*

"I'm living the life everyone wants to lead and trapped living the life no one wants. Our nightmares come as often as the dreams. The voices call me crazy. They call me genius. They hold me down. They don't understand. I live all realities. I live all dreams. I live all nightmares. I feel fire, gunshots, and broken bones, violated, stabbed, punched, kicked. I feel hate. I feel love. I feel rich. I feel poor. I feel happy. I feel sad. I feel anger. I feel life. I feel death. I feel... I feel... I feel... The spirit of being. I feel all possibilities. The line between dreams and reality, I feel it all. Any image the human mind can conjure becomes my reality. I live the dreams. I live the nightmares. I feel it all at the same time in the same moment in the limitlessness of being.

"I remember being normal. I was a child when They revealed themselves to me. I am one of Them. They took my ability to communicate with the voices. They know I'm going to tell. I've been to the home place. No room for life now. It's dark. We feel each other out. This primitive world can't dream. My family figures I'm better off here. They visit, but they don't stay. When they are here I hear only silence: no dreams, no nightmares, silence. Voice is not the means through which we speak. We move without sound. They tell me someday I'll be able to go home but they never give me a date. I don't understand how they can watch me die, a little more every day. How do you watch a thing like this? For my silence? For my thoughts? For my ideas? For my hopes? For my dreams? I am blessed away into the fire. They burn the body around my spirit with time; they desire to kill my identity.

"My experience is spent looking through a window of change. I exist because of existence. No life. No death. Only the state of being. The endless state of being one with All is all there is, all that has ever been, and all that will ever be. Be a part in the endless evolution of life. Be something different than there was before. Close your eyes and feel the presence of being one with All. It is prayer: the time of sleep. You touch this place when you close your eyes. Brain waves tap

31

in like a computer and you enter the essence of being thoughts. Your existence is only a state of mind.

"Imagine an eternity locked in a state of being all things at once, never knowing single-subject reality. With no distinction multiple realities merge together. Do you see me in your reality? Our moments exist together. When I see you, you are different than you are in your mind. In my eyes, you will not be what you think you are.

"I heard a voice that sounded like a trumpet. It told me the universe I see is already gone. It told me I live in the past, that I live one second behind the universe. *One second behind the universe? I questioned. How am I one with all and yet I'm a second behind the present? This means separation. How is there separation when I am one with All?* The trumpet voice blared loudly in my mind; the energy of anger and frustration resonating in its sound.

"I'll never forget the message I received as the voice said, 'The future is shrouded in darkness because it is in a constant state of creation. Born of formlessness, the future exists in limitless possibilities, while the past can only exist in completion. You are a second behind the universe because the future must be created. Collective energy creates the future. The moment is continual. The moment is all we have. In the moment you are one with all, but you live in the reflection of completed past.'

"I heard the voice loud in my heart. The deafening sound burned into my mind. I am a creation, no matter my state. I am the moment. One second behind formlessness. The future. I paused in my revelations, there's something missing... *What is life?*

"Silence. The quiet signaled what seemed a non-response.

"I asked my question again, *What is life? If the past is creation, the moment is existence, and the future is formless – what is life?*

"Silence persisted, confounding me. The uncomfortable sound of my own insecurities: silence. Echoes of my fears and worries: silence. Endless questions without answers: silence. Endless problems without solutions: silence. Finally the trumpet voice sounded, softer and more soothing.

"'Life is the existence of all things, the energy that always is, only taking form to be. Life's past: creation; life's moment: existence; and life's future: limitless possibilities all One. No new energy ever added and none taken away; there is only transference. This is life.'

"The answer was an obvious revelation. Life is an energy which has always existed in one form or another. This energy, our energy, has always been. All of the elements to create me, to create earth, the sun, the solar system, have always existed in some form or another. One with All, from one existence. I had one final question. I was afraid of what the answer might be. The all-knowing trumpet voice could offer revelation, but this revelation is one that a life isn't meant to know.

"*What is death*? I braced myself for the answer.

"Annoyance erupted from the trumpet voice. High-pitched tones streaked across my mind and drove tears from my eyes with excruciating pain.

"'Death is the transference! In life, one moment is always existence. The energy is always existence. Your death is a transition. The energy cannot be contained it must roam free. Death is the transference!'

"All of my fears previously captured in a single word: *death*. I always thought it to be the end but life never ends, life never began it will always be: the energy. Everything that's ever been created came from the moment. This moment has always been. This moment is always there. The past is created and the future is formless. This moment is the true form of existence. A welcomed silence fell and the trumpet voice allowed me to sleep."

Chapter V: The First Subject

Fears can prevent us from learning and progressing. I wasn't afraid of the answers until I knew they existed. The fear of being found keeps me hidden in a web of darkness. This life seems normal, but this way is not mine. Who I am and what I am are two different things. I am a scientist by study and trade, but I'm in a world that doesn't fit me. I play a role for an audience I do not know, on a stage I'd rather not be on. My students look to me for instruction, waiting for me to perform the role and play this part. I can barely remember my lines. Fear. How do I get past fear? What lies past fear?

Today I must take them to see the first subject, a subject given to me by the Underground. Her name is Maria. She was a scientist like me. She was brilliant with a career poised for greatness. Until now, I had no idea she'd been captured by the Protectors. I wanted to free her, but they told me rescuing her could jeopardize the Underground's safety. Though my face is different now, they can still find me.

I look forward to seeing her again. I wonder if she still thinks of me. I prepare for a difficult task. I was briefed on her condition. What happened? A very big day for us was now here.

The maximum-security hospital's smell of sterilized walls and floors, deodorized carpets and cooking food mingle through the air into my senses. My students follow behind me. To them this was just an activity for their class. Ms. Emch and Mr. Macpherson both look distracted. Mr. Macpherson is impatient and hurried, as if things were moving too slowly. Ms. Emch appears irritated, as if there is something she hasn't quite figured out how to take care of yet. Ms. Thick chats with Mr. LaDay about unrelated social issues, something about the President of the United States. Ms. Amen is taking things more seriously than the rest of them. Her eyes survey every inch of the hospital as we walk.

Dr. Mace, Maria's doctor, meets us in the lobby of the hospital. The students all focus their attention when he enters the room. He greets us with handshakes, asking our names. Is he one of them?

Orderlies, the hospital's version of security, come next; large, muscular men with ugly faces. No handshaking with them. They escort us to the wing of the hospital were Maria is being held. It is dimly lit. We are below ground. She's been here for years. She was once a brilliant scientist, one of the greatest minds in the world. Now she's a patient who can't remember her own identity. Dr. Mace briefs us on her condition before opening the door:

Maria Rivera, forty-nine-years old, developed an undifferentiated type of schizophrenia when she was in her late 20's. Her positive symptoms, such as disturbances in sensation, delusions, and false perceptions, were not serious at the time of her original diagnosis. She had, however, shown stronger initial signs of severely disorganized thought processes, speech, and behavior. The severity of these symptoms were attributed to her work overload. *Lies.*

She was the top student in her class at an Ivy League university. *Truth.* Although her behavior was irregular, she showed no signs of loss of motivation. Still the top student in her class, she was prescribed medication to help her cope with her lighter symptoms. Her treatment showed strong initial signs of improvement; a minimizing of her array of disorganized behavior. Her response to the treatment caused the doctors to believe that she didn't suffer from schizophrenia at all. It was swept under the rug as obsessive compulsive disorder and acute stress. *Lies.*

Maria went on to lead a normal life until a few years ago when more severe symptoms appeared. She experienced an acute reduction in normal functioning. She began to slip at work. Her emotional reactions were first to show signs: she was happy when she heard bad news and sad when she heard good news. She displayed no emotional response to seeing friends and family. Then the delusions began. She developed a belief that she was an alien conceived by alien parents. She believed her life to be false, insisting she was sent to Earth as punishment by her home world. Her senses became disoriented. She felt cold when it was hot; she felt stab wounds, and cuts from which there was no injury. She would cry out that her skin was on fire. She stopped responding to her own name. Instead, she began referring to herself as "Vida". She began to demonstrate delusions of reference, convinced everyone who spoke was talking to her or about her: the other patients in the hospital, their visitors, the newscaster on TV, the radio announcer. Songs became coded messages from her home world. Billboard advertisements held secret meanings. She began to hear voices and lost touch with objective reality altogether. Her ideas and her words slurred affecting her speech to the point that she has become nonsensical to the listener. Maria is the worst case Dr. Mace has ever seen.

The door to the observation cell is covered by thick steel plating, secured with heavy metal bolts. A small window serves as the peephole through the massive reinforced door. Maria lay motionless on the floor. She's dressed in a white hospital gown and straitjacket. She's sleeping. Her hair, still as long and luxurious as I remember, is matted to her face in a violent disarray of sweat and saliva. She looks cold, shivering as she sleeps. The blue straitjacket is the only color in the barren white room. My heart sinks seeing her in this condition, remembering her vibrant and full of life.

Dr. Mace has no idea I knew her. Dr. Mace has no idea I know the diagnosis from her previous doctor was incorrect. This was revenge from the Protectors. Maria had never seen a psychiatrist in college much less been diagnosed with obsessive-compulsive disorder and stress. I know because I was with her in college. We graduated in the same class. We took the same courses and had the same internships; when Maria went to work at the laboratory, I went with her. She was my best friend. Yes, there is a lot Dr. Mace doesn't know about Maria. Still, they had to know I would come for her. They had to know I felt guilty for abandoning her. I didn't know how else to protect her. I figured if I left, there would be no reason for them to harm her. I knew she would be hurt but it was the only thing I could do. I never told Maria the Truth; I only left her a letter stating that I had to leave due to circumstances beyond my control. I wanted her to know that I loved her and she would always be in my heart. It was for her own good. When the broadcast news issued the alert to find me I was horrified by what she would think. Still, I felt it was best. I was gone and she was

36

safe. I can't tell her what happened or about my plan; they have ways of finding out if someone is lying or hiding something. As I look into this room at the shell of the woman I once knew, I wonder if I made the right choice to stay away. Here the woman I love lays broken because of my love for her. My wife. How could I not come back for my wife? I have to save her.

I fight off tears by digging my thumbnail into my index finger. The doctor leads me into the cell. The students go to a room where they can observe via the hospital's closed circuit monitoring system. I am in another world. Dr. Mace is talking. Maria is prone to fits of violent rage due to her psychosis. I don't remember feeling my feet touch the ground from outside the steel door to standing inches in front of her. I kneel down to touch her, her hair, her hand, anything. She's snatched from my reach by several staff who followed us into the room. They place her on a bed. She shows no response to their actions. Her body is limp. No emotion. The only visible sign that she is awake are her emerald green eyes shining brightly. No emotion.

No signs of struggle. No resistance. They strap her down. Dr. Mace assures me it is policy and for our own safety, as well as hers. He said he protested the request for this patient because the hospital had still not been able to pinpoint a diagnosis of schizophrenia. Normally, the University requests patients with less severe diagnoses. However, after a thorough evaluation of my credentials, he changed his mind and granted our request. I look up. The camera's alien eye uploading our interaction.

My wife's fingers, always so well kept, now bore ragged nails bitten to the nubs, frayed cuticles, and tiny cuts. Even in her current state I see beauty as she begins to move. The drugs were taking their affect. Her eyes roll back, but she doesn't move. Tears well behind my eyes as I find it difficult to breathe. I want to unstrap her from the cold steel bed, pick her up in my arms, and carry us both away from this horrible mess. She begins to blink, her lashes flutter and her eyes roll frantically grasping to find reality. Her mouth is slack. Her once luscious lips, caked with crust in the corners, are dry and chapped.

"Good... morning," she says, her voice hoarse and cracking.

37

"Good morning," I respond.

She flexes her muscles to stretch in her restraints. Her body writhing and squirming. Her movements trigger my memory and I am transported.

We stayed for a month at a cabin on Lake Tahoe enjoying rest and relaxation during a brief work-free moment in our lives. We imagined a beautiful life together as we shared our goals and plans. She dreamed of retiring and traveling the world. I dreamed of retiring and writing while we travelled together. I remember those early mornings watching her stretch as she parted her beautiful eyelashes -- treasure chests covering the reward of her emerald eyes. My thumbnail into my index finger pulls from those eyes through space and time. In a waking nightmare watching the woman I love struggle to be alive.

"Sorry I'm up so late baby. I was doing a lot of research." She looks at me, her eyes dart away. "Baby! Baby! Where are you? Who are these men? Where is my husband? Where's my husband?"

Straining against the leather restraints with furious motions she screams. She screams my name.

"Adam! Adam! Adam! ...Adam!"

Over and over she screams. Gut wrenching screams. All I can do is stand here and watch as the staff work to calm her. A nurse enters with a syringe. She sticks the needle in Maria's arm and finally, in sedation, she begins to relax and her screams turn to whispers. She continues to say my name, slowly, deliberately, like a chant of affirmation. Then, she falls silent.

Dr. Mace explains that this is a regular occurrence. The only times they have been able to study her are when she's alone or heavily sedated. He says her episodes always begin with her husband Adam. A man who, as far as they can tell, never existed. I ask Dr. Mace what happened to her family. He tells me that her mother, father, and brother were killed shortly before her admittance to the hospital during a family ski trip. They went missing for over a week. Their bodies were found buried in an avalanche. Dr. Mace went on, saying she rarely mentions her family, but in every recorded observation she's trying called out to her husband, Adam.

This doctor doesn't distinguish outside what he reads. Here a woman is calling out for a man named as her husband and the doctor dismisses it as a delusional reference because it is not part of her background report. The fiery urge to grab him and shake into him some sense of human nature rose within me. I want to scream, *I am Adam you book fed fool programmed with degrees for a certified practice. She is my wife, put here because of me. Because of my choice to leave, my choice to abandon her.*

Instead, I stare at my wife, sleeping silently. I want to kiss her cheek as I have done countless times. I turn my head away and silently kiss her in my mind. *I will come back for you my love.* I say goodbye to Dr. Mace and tell him we will be back to continue tomorrow.

I drink alone. It has been a while since I've had a drink. My beloved Maria. The liquor soothes my wounds. Each sip brings me closer to acceptance. I am responsible for my wife's condition. The sips meant to numb my wounds begin to feed my rage and focus my anger. It was the Protectors who inflicted these wounds, they are the essence of my dilemma. I throw the room's only lamp against the wall. In darkness I cry.

Maria and I had been happy. At the time I chose to leave her, my decision seemed selfless. I wanted her to be happy and have a life free of this. I didn't want to drag her through the turmoil and uncertainty she would have to endure with me. The love we shared could have endured those obstacles, and still I chose to leave. Had I just served the needs of the Protectors we would not be here now in this place of uncertainty. She would be with me and I would not be in this false world created to mask who I really am. I would be me. I may not have been happy with the works of the Protectors, but I would have spent my life with Maria. After seeing her today, I would gladly serve them well. How could I have been so foolish as to think she'd be alright without me? No man could ever love her like me and she could never love another as she loves me. She still calls my name. Every fiber of me ached to answer her, but I couldn't, not yet.

I don't care what it takes. I want to honor my vow and take her away from all of this. My wife. My students and I will have to devise a way to get through to her, we have to make contact.

Chapter VI: Breakthrough

In my office, hung-over from the night before, I watch the empty classroom fill with students. The monitor on my desk transmits images from a hidden camera. In first walked Mr. LaDay, with Ms. Emch moments behind him. Seeing them made me hopeful. Ten-minutes remained before class. Ingesting my breakfast a coffee with a few antacids, last night's escapade with my deepest emotions lingered in my thoughts. Finally Ms. Thick then Mr. Macpherson entered the classroom on my monitor. The students engage in casual, groggy morning conversations. Slowly the conversation veers toward the previous day's observations of our subject.

Ms. Thick: "How are we supposed to help that lady when she can't stay conscious without heavy emotion suppression medication?"

Mr. LaDay: "We just need to let her freak out and see what happens."

Ms. Emch: "She could hurt herself or somebody else in the room. It's not safe. We can't do that!"

Mr. LaDay: "At least we'll have a better idea of how to help her if she hurts herself. Sedating her will never allow us to know what's really going on in her head."

Ms. Emch: "It's too dangerous."

Mr. LaDay: "Well how do you propose we analyze her? What do we do? Just watch her while she lies still and hope she does something we can study?"

Ms. Emch: "No, that's not what I'm saying."

Mr. LaDay: "Then what are you saying?"

Mr. Macpherson: "Danny, if you'd let her talk long enough maybe you'd find out."

Mr. LaDay: "Look Wes, this is not football; you don't run this class."

Mr. Macpherson: "Why don't you shut up and listen for once, Danny. Deb, what are you saying?"

Ms. Emch: "Just forget about it. I'm here to learn. You guys do whatever and I'm in. If it doesn't work, at least I'll learn from it. That's what's important to me."

Ms. Thick: "Deb, nobody runs this class. We are here for each other. No matter who says what."

Mr. LaDay: "What the hell is that supposed to mean? What is this? Jump on Danny day? I'm just trying to come up with something to help this woman, and now I'm trying to teach the class?"

Mr. Macpherson: "What were you going to say, Deb? We want to know."

Mr. LaDay: "Yeah, please tell us what you think."

She smirked visibly enough for the camera to pick up and display on the monitor in my office.

Ms. Emch: "Well, we should do a little more research on the subject's background. I don't think the husband is a figment of her imagination. There has got to be a reason why she keeps bringing this Adam person up."

The angry words of provoked thought inspire genius activity.

Ms. Thick: "Deb, I'm not a private investigator. I didn't sign up for that."

Ms. Emch: "I know Tracie, but we must have sufficient history on our patients. We can't just assume because we can't talk to the patient and gather information the hospital lacks. We are going to have to do a little digging. That's research, Tracie, not investigation."

The students, so engaged in their conversation, don't notice Ms. Amen's arrival. She watches them, writes something down and then walks to Mr. Macpherson. An interesting choice. The group pays her little attention. She startles Mr. Macpherson, smiling at his flinch and hands him the slip of paper.

Mr. Macpherson: "Hold on! Hold on. I have something from Geraldine... *Why don't we do both?*"

The group falls silent, my cue to enter the room. They turn to acknowledge my presence.

"Class, we will divide into two teams; Mrs. Amen is right. Ms. Emch and Mr. Macpherson will research background information. Ms.

Thick and Mr. LaDay will help implement new interview strategy. No medication – this time.

"Background information team, I want you two to research all public documentation on the subject and look for things that don't match up with the hospital's records. Ms. Amen, you will observe both teams' progress and be involved in bridging our findings."

The students agree without question. I dismiss the class.

We enter the hospital amidst stares and whispers from conspicuous staff. Maybe I am being paranoid, but they seem to be watching us. I'm not sure if it is my anxiety, paranoia, nervousness, or maybe a combination playing a part in my assessment. I don't know whose eyes are whose, I just know I feel their eyes on me. Contact with Maria is surely being investigated. The Protectors are here somewhere. They could have done away with her and she'd have never been found, easily becoming one of the many missing persons who disappear from their place in society every day. A finely crafted story would have sealed their actions. She'd have vanished into thin air. The protectors knew what they were doing when they placed her here. In my disguise they can't see me. If they knew it was me, I'd have been apprehended. How could they have known to put Maria in this city under these circumstances? She's a secret patient in a maximum-security hospital. Of all the cities in this country, she was placed here. She was placed within twenty miles of me, and we were thousands of miles from where we once worked. Was it my profile that led them to believe I'd be here? Did their knowledge of my likes and dislikes tell them this is where I'd ended up? Or did I find her by a stroke of destiny or luck? I know the best minds in the country are at their disposal. I'd removed the tracking device implanted in my thigh, so how did they know I was here? How did they know I'd find out she was here? I'd left her with them. They assume I'd be able to reach her. I'd made no contact with her whatsoever. They knew that. So what made them think I'd even care that I lost her? It isn't just my thoughts, the staff is staring at me; they've been waiting for me. A message to the Underground; they wanted me to find her.

Dr. Mace greets us with an enthusiastic smile, inappropriate for the situation at hand. Today we plan to evaluate Maria without any medication or interference whatsoever. Beads of sweat glide across skin, short breath, chills from gut; more sweat. My students breaking into groups, comfort. I doubt my ability to remain objective. Giving Mr. LaDay and Ms. Thick the job of evaluation, observation, and strategic planning allows me some presence of mind. They're watching me from the observation area advising me through an earpiece. Ms. Amen remains with me in the session. She will communicate with me using her notepad. I'd conferred with Dr. Mace ahead of time about our new strategy for evaluating Maria. He was resistant, stating he's attempted evaluations of Maria under similar circumstances, but they didn't work. Her positive symptoms consumed her. Her hallucinations, false perceptions, and delusions severely affected her thought process; he feared she could go into cardiac arrest or suffer a stroke. He told us that in one session she'd scratched flesh from her arms in an attempt to rid herself of the costume she feels disguised in. She believes her body is a vessel imprisoning her real form. The only way to free herself is to destroy the body. From that session on she'd been placed in a straitjacket during all non-medicated sessions. He attempted to evaluate her using the non-medicated strategy a few more times before abandoning it for safer and more tempered measures. Today, he smiles as he greets us. Why was he so happy when he didn't agree with us? Grossly inappropriate. That smile. Against his wishes, we are to evaluate Maria's non-sedated, non-medicated behavior. He insists Maria be restrained during the session. I am against it, but concede on the fairness of give and take.

I enter the observation room with three of my five students. The others remain in contact using a direct frequency line to the observation room. If they find any pertinent information they will contact us simultaneously by way of holographic images observed through optical lenses they wear. My support system in place, I stand before the door, ready to see the love of my life.

We step into her padded observation cell. Heavily restrained I feel her in the reflection of a single tear. My mental restraints reflected in her physical ones. A picture painted by a monster. Her wrists, her elbows, her shoulders, her waist, her knees, her ankles, her forehead all strapped to a steel bed with leather restraints. Like the spirit inside me she lay motionless, even her tears unable to move toward what she wants. My beloved. I wish to cradle her away from all of this, free us from these hate filled barriers. My knees... to remain standing requires concentration. Somehow, I summon the strength to move another step. I don't remember walking, but now I know the reason he gave such a smile. This gut wrenching portrait of procedural measures was coveted behind his grin; a twisted pleasure to receive from these conditions. She whispers to herself unaware of our entrance into the observation cell. I listen as she mutters. I can make out her words. "Ten-oh-three... ten-oh-three..." Over and over again she says this mantra. I find comfort: she still remembers the month and day we met. It eased my nerves.

"Baby, I'm here."

The haze of medication still evident in her gaze. Through years of pain she reaches to understand the situation before her. My face is different. She looks into my eyes. Tears driving lanes rapidly down her face.

"Adam? Adam, baby? It hurts Adam. Where have you been? Where have you been, baby? Why did you leave? It hurts so bad. Why?"

She projected the love in my eyes. I had to stay professional.

"What hurts? What's hurting you?"

"The fire baby. It burns. It holds me down. They showed me our true image. We're formless and then with starlight they set me on fire."

"I don't... I don't see flames on your skin. You look... normal." I lied.

"No. It's not fire you see. It's fire you feel. Prisons we call bodies holding us captive in times of reflection. A measure of place formed in observed existence a moment of space. The truth of existence evades our understanding because time traps us in limited thinking. Time of life between birth and death enslaves us into diminished conceptions of perceiving the galaxies after solar systems. Nights and days, spins of planets. Neither night nor day exists in the universe, only movement and creation. The transference of energy. It hurts to be separated from our essential spirit. My flesh burns."

"Maria, you speak of a home world. Have you been here all your life? Are you of Earth?"

Across those lips she spread a devilish grin. Laughing, her eyes became crazed rolling beams of excitement. From the corner of her mouth a thread of saliva dripped. She giggled at the home world question.

"My love, I see the truth, has only been revealed to you in a small portion. I guess that's why you're not here like me."

She aimed her rolling eyes toward the camera lens observing us.

"I speak of a home world because we are not from here! Yes, like everyone else I was born on Earth with energy born of another place trapped in a prison of light. The home is where our energy is free to exist as thoughts. Not a planet, it's a place of formlessness where single units form energy interaction, millions of thoughts concentrate into belief and birth the actions of physical form."

"You want to be in a place that doesn't exist?"

"I want to end this form. I don't want to be a part of this. Inside ourselves, we are energy which wishes to form existence. They want to change the universe and infect it with limited perceptions. The Originals placed us here. Gods."

"Do you trust that information as truth?"

She laughed, louder with a sharper, piercing pitch. Seeing a woman like this – laughing strapped down to a bed unable to even move her head, tears welling in her eyes, my stomach cringes as hot prickles in my chest, arms, legs and loins.

"How can I possibly believe this?" She cried, "You want know how, Adam? Because after you left me pregnant with our child, They took me and told me everything. They showed me the Truth. They showed me what made you run away!"

"What... What did They show you Maria?"

46

"The same thing They showed you: our path. They showed me how They control minds. They showed me how They release new ideas that seem invented: impulses sent out to receptive minds. The right frequency life observer captures the impulse and chooses to react to the thoughts. They release the impulse constantly until it is born into formal belief. Don't you wonder why inventions are hurried into existence by more than one mind? It's Them. They are doing this. The impulses sent out by the Controllers, are smaller than the smallest things, Gods the master family of all humans. They're not like us, Adam. They've known for millennia. We don't die, we transition. The transference: death and rebirth. The cycle between birth and death holds us captive. The smallest the largest, who gives them invention and direction? Through invention we build and create what They need to infect the universe."

It was too much to hear. She'd gone into another state of mind. How can anyone fully understand another dimension of perception? The mentally insane try to perceive our dimension of reality.

She said she was pregnant. I didn't know.

"Maria, why do They wish to infect the universe?"

"Oh, Adam, my love. You know better than anybody why. They wish to control the universe. They want to be Gods. It's all in the Book of Books. We live inside ourselves. The smallest and largest are one thing. Formlessness to the world of shape. The world of appearances. As we travel the universe, we travel inside ourselves. As we travel inside ourselves, we travel inside the energy of creation. That is the formula to control the formlessness of creation. We, they, us, our energy becomes one with All. The winds of thoughts blowing us about and choosing our stops in space and time. We control the form."

"Maria, if we all are a part of the same energy, 'one with All', then how can one individual part control all of the energy?"

"Adam, I just told you. Formlessness creates form. An idea, born in the mind, is formless. The idea manifests through physical action. Everything around you originated in the essence of thought. The mind and everything you see, is the answer to everything."

47

"Maria, someone's mind did not create everything around us. Trees, water, air, and mountains are natural things here before us. The mind did not create nature."

"How do you know, Adam? How do you know? Let's say you don't know the truth, and I know you know the truth, but let's just say, for argument sake, you don't and all of this is too complex for you to understand. I'd like to ask you a question."

"What is it?"

"Come here, honey, it's a secret. Let me whisper it to you."

I look away from her to Ms. Amen for assurance. I hesitated in obeying a command from my own wife. I was unsure of her, strapped to that bed, her hair matted in disarray, her eyes crazed. She wasn't seeing the world I was seeing. We weren't living in the same reality. She called me honey. We had a baby. I bend down to hear her question. With slithering speed and a venomous tongue she whispers into my ear.

"Look at all of this. All of these things created before you were born into this physical body, Adam. This bed, this room, the lights, the windows, the design of clothing: you accept these things as man-made because that's what they told you. They trick you with foreign nature. Aliens! How do you know it's real when you only know what they tell you? They tell you how to learn, how to read. They program you from birth. Your beliefs were passed on from your guardians and others who were here before you. They taught you to believe in the human condition. That's how powerful the mind is. The idea. The idea controls your actions. The idea controls your beliefs. The idea really does control life. We live in a world of ideas you can see. Ideas born from the mind all around you. They appear in the blink of an eye and assume a life of their own. Think about the first light bulb created. Now, where are light bulbs? They're everywhere. The first plane. The first car. The first train. All those things created before you were born. Now, you decide to question your wife? You don't believe me when I tell you all things are created from the idea out of formlessness and through creation, the formless idea materializes in the world of appearances? *This is the world of appearances, Adam*. The world where the mind exists in the universe and the universe is the mind, the thought, the idea."

"Maria, don't believe this vast universe, this planet, those mountains, those stars, my existence… don't believe I don't matter. Where does that question begin, where does it end."

"Sweetheart, that's not my question.""What is your question, Maria?"

"Come closer."

I move in.

She screams, "How do you know, Adam? How do you know it's not real? You only think how they tell you to think! You think it's natural to be buried in the ground or burned to ash, don't you, Adam? You're one of them! You're one of them! You're not my husband!"

She spit on me with the seriousness of her words.

Hospital staff rush in with Dr. Mace. Ms. Amen and I are quickly ushered from Maria to the room where Mr. LaDay and Ms. Thick wait. Maria's voice now only over loud speaker through the new room in which I find myself standing.

Dr. Mace silences her cries, but I could still see her on the monitor. He shuts it off completing the process of taking her away from me.

"Professor!"

His voice pulled me back into reality.

"Professor, this is a breakthrough! We can reconvene in the morning to discuss new strategy. This is amazing!"

He took my wife. She knows I'm out here. She can't find me. I was talking to her for the first time in years. This doctor that tied her to the bed is talking to me about strategy. I flex in my mental restraints.

"How dare you interrupt a session! That patient was on the brink of an even greater breakthrough and you stopped us. Now we have to start over and re-implement our strategy. As a fellow professional, you should be ashamed of yourself. There was no reason for you to end that session. I was in control of the patient and she was properly restrained! Do you hear me? *She was properly restrained!*"

49

My fists were clinched around his button-up shirt and his feet were almost off the ground. My students rushed to disconnect me from the source of my rage.

"Professor! What has gotten into you? That was uncalled for!"

"Uncalled for? Uncalled for? You restrain her like some animal! She had no way to harm herself or anyone else. Yet, you felt the need to terminate my session? There will be a strategic meeting with you in the morning. My students and I will return here resume our work, and tomorrow you will be more professional than you were today. You will allow us to continue our session uninterrupted and allow our university to continue with our research. Are we clear, doctor?" I snarled, "Are we clear?"

Gritting his teeth, "Yes… Yes, Professor. We are clear."

"Good, doctor. I'm glad."

My students and I leave the building to plan our next session. We needed the answers that would come from analyzing what she said. We talked for hours. To them, her ramblings are those of a mentally unstable woman; her words representing opportunity to dig deeper inside her psychosis. Their understanding confined to students of the mind, not students of experience.

When I return home I open a bottle of scotch and drink more than I have ever before. With no food in my stomach, I attempt to pace myself with two-ounce shots. At night's end the bottle is empty and I have received my de facto therapy for the choices I've made. The outlet to express my dilemma.

Amidst chaos, I awake. Papers, books, clothes strewn throughout the room. Furniture overturned and out of place. Everything in disarray. The classical music set for my alarm tries to soothe me. I pry myself off the stairs leading to my room. My head throbs from dehydration, the remnants of my intoxication lingering heavily in my system. I'm still drunk stepping into the shower. I want to cleanse myself of the previous day. The water washing away the dirt I feel on my filthy skin. I can't wash away the filth on my spirit. A grime that buries me deep in a grave I've dug alone. Now I must live here as a clone.

My students are waiting for me when I arrive at the hospital. They've been waiting almost twenty minutes. I'm not late. I am ten minutes early. They are eager to begin our next evaluation. Mr. Macpherson and Ms. Emch depart to the county records department to investigate something they've discovered in Maria's college background. In the records she's listed as confidential clearance. We will compare records with interviews.

A smile does not accompany Dr. Mace's greeting today. Apologizing for yesterday he assures us that today he will not interfere. Ms. Amen, Mr. LaDay, Mrs. Thick and I review Maria's chart for her behavior overnight. She's been sedated and sleeps most of the day. Only waking once to walk in a circle three times, then go back to bed. Odd, but not alarming. Dr. Mace informs us she is unrestrained except for a straitjacket. I ask for one arm freed. He agrees. He asks if we want to observe her behavior before going inside. We decline. He opens the door. She is sitting in the corner of the room rocking back and forth with one arm holding her knees. Again she is whispering something. She looks up. The door closes behind us. I begin.

"Maria, how are you doing?"

She looks at me curiously, like an animal inspecting a newly-discovered object in its domain. She smiles then speaks,

"You have eyes like my husband. Did you know this is the third civilization?"

"I'm not sure I know what you mean."

She raises from of her rocking trance and begins to walk. She moves, looking away from me, tracing the padded walls with her finger.

"The third civilization? We've done this before, Adam. The last civilization existed for 10,000 years. The Protectors of the largest were almost wiped out. They learned to control the weather. Imagine the power that comes from being able to control and change weather. Floods, hurricanes, tornados, endless storms, wind, and snow, all tools at your disposal. The weather wiped them out, buried them with

51

layers and layers of sands from time and place volcanoes erupted. Another ice age. Several volcanoes exploded at once shifting Earth one degree. The lava wipes out civilizations and the ice age causes separations of generations – the eraser of history. We don't know of their existence."

"Maria, how? If we exist now, then some of us survived and those who survived would have known and carried on in the memory of the past civilization. There couldn't have been a lost era of humanity before this one."

She approaches me with a smile, still running her finger against the thick rubber wall. Ms. Amen looks at me with concern. As though looking for something on the wall Maria's eyes are focused on her tracing finger. Only a few feet from me, she takes her finger from the frame of the room and traces through the air, drawing shapes toward me. I jump a little when she stops in front of me. Smiling at my fear, she places her free hand on my chest, over my heart.

"A chromosome up, a syndrome down, is our mutation to survive the elements of nature without human comforts of invention. Civilization, culture, is the characteristic of a time or place. Civilization represents cultural and technological development. Some of the population survived, but thousands of years separated the growth of historical civilizations' connection. Those who survived could not carry on the traditions and customs of the last civilization. Humans must adapt. The harsh environment forces them to abandon their ways and adopt new ones. Honey, you are so adorable now."

She takes her palm from my heart and puts her middle finger to her lips.

"Shhh... They can hear your heartbeat."

"Who can hear my heartbeat, Maria?"

She laughs.

"The people who sent you, honey."

She walks back toward the wall outstretching her arm... Back and forth her grasping palm as if squeezing something unseen; clasping nothing as she spoke.

"The people who sent you and the people who brought you are two different groups with the same intentions. I truly wish..."

She stops and points up toward the camera whispering, "There they are... See that? That's how they watch us. They want to know what I know. That's why you're here."

"Maria, you said they showed you the truth. If that's true what difference does it make what you know? They have you captive."

"Adam, my dear husband," she lifts her gown, slightly exposing herself. "I know you. You are a threat to them. You think they don't know you're part of the revelation? They know. You are the one they are afraid of. What you saw, what you learned, is more than anyone outside has ever known and now you're free. The only reason they don't kill you right now is because they have a plan. I'm not sure what that plan is, but you can rest assured it has something to do with me and you, and the protection of those secrets."

She came close to me, still holding her gown, exposing her beautiful body. Once near me she grabs my hand and places it on her body. Her sweet backside molded into my grip.

"Do you remember me, Adam? Do you remember how we used to make love endlessly through the night? I miss you baby. How could you leave me? Every night I lay in bed alone touching myself thinking of you. How could you walk away?"

I wanted to pull away but she held my hands, moving them along her smooth, soft flesh. Oh... how I remember. I forced myself to pull away.

"Maria, my love, why would I want to walk away from you? They were..."

"They were out to get you. Yes. I know."

She moves away from me, toward the door. A chill from her absent touch races up my spine.

"Does that mean you couldn't have taken me with you? It's okay, we are together now and that's what's important. I know you aren't going to leave me this time, Adam. I always knew you couldn't stay away. I always knew you would come back to me."

She sat, Indian-style, with her one free arm cupped in front of the door.

"They knew you'd come back too. That's why we're here. Now, where was I? Oh, the civilization. Super-humans existed on Earth. I know it sounds crazy in those words. *Super-human* a fantastic term that takes realism away. The mind associates super-humans with any number of different fantasy stories or movies. It's hard for us to relate, but that is what they are, super. They communicate on a much higher level without using words. Traveling light speed living a life which bends and warps the time in human existence. They are different. A light year is thousands of years on Earth. Older generations of humans and newer generations of humans can be the same age at the same time in space, causing generational non-existence for those aliens with the perception of Gods. Some are the same age, yet born in different generations. Think about that, Adam. Does it sound familiar to you? They chase life through time, living centuries and only aging a few years, they rejuvenate life using stem cells. Any organ can be completely replaced through a reorganization process; the ability to rejuvenate specific portions of the body to any specific age. Age differences are irrelevant for people who live unlimited amounts of time. Death of form becomes almost non-existent. Objects move with minds. Expanding existence. Sound familiar, darling?"

I knew what she was speaking of. I'd heard it before. I decided to change direction.

"Vida!"

Her eyes lit up. Again she rocked back and forth in front of the door. A wide-eyed smile grew across her face.

"Vida! Why are we so far behind those who came before us in understanding and technology?"

She rocks with increasing speed, her eyes unblinking, lips still smiling.

"Adam, my love. I was wondering when you'd call me by my real name."

Leaping quickly to her feet, she paces in front of the door. She stops, looks at me then Ms. Amen with a raised eyebrow.

"They do not want us to have their power. They govern us. They move us. As slaves, we are beneath them. They put us here. They colonized this planet."

"Vida, I need to change direction because I'm having difficulty understanding something. If this is about us, why do other life forms exist? What's their purpose?"

A wonderful performance for my students. I knew the lines she'd speak.

"Adam, our lives, all lives, are dependent on energy. Energy feeds on energy redistributing a finite amount. We only recycle and discover energy already in place. When we consume life forms we release the energy for another life to take the place of form in the space of that moment: existence observed reflection experienced through space time impressions of ego. The cycle of life; one species flourishes, another species goes extinct -- the delicate balance of nature."

She walks closer to me and puts her middle and index fingers on my right temple. She massages my mind in waves. The motion calms me. She takes my hand. Standing face to face, looking deep into my eyes, after countless moons of missing her reflection. My wife speaks to me.

"What separates us from other life forms? Our mind. The human mind has the ability to create illusions in reality. The human mind is one of the most powerful energy forms of life. The ability to understand the complexities of other forms and make those complexities work on our behalf. We create our dreams and that is important for us to preserve. I'm sure your glimpse of their works was enough to make you aware, but do you know? My mind has been poisoned with this, lover. I can no longer function in society. How do you do it, baby? As are you, I am alien. You know what it's like. You act like a normal person, but you are not like them. You know why we slave. You know what all of this is for. Tell me, Adam, what's your favorite television program?"

She kisses my cheek letting go of my hand. Away from me she walks back toward the door. Facing away she repeats her question,

"What's your favorite television program, love? What do you watch?"

Silent, I couldn't think of a television program, not one show. She knew I couldn't watch it. I know what it is. I know what it does. I know what it's for. I needed to say *something*.

"I'm a very busy man, Maria. I'm a college professor. My time for watching television is limited. I barely have time to get dressed in the morning. Watching television is not on my agenda."

She turns I'm caught in my excitement to see her... Her face twisted in anger.

"Liar! You know why you don't do it! You don't watch it for the same reason we all don't. You want it to stop. You want to block it out. You don't want to be reminded of the duty. Liar! Liar!"

She began beating on the door.

"Dr. Mace! Dr. Mace! This is not my husband."

I reach out to her. She pulls away.

"I don't want to see you. I want to sleep. Go away, liar!"

Dr. Mace and his staff appear in the looking glass of the steel door. The door slides open and two staff members escort Maria away. I look at Ms. Amen. Dr. Mace looks at me,

"Would you like me to end the session now, Professor? Or do you want me to bring her back out?"

Chapter VII: A New Approach

In the lecture hall Mr. Macpherson and Ms. Emch share what they found in the county records. I expected it to be only things directly about my beloved. Instead, it includes something about Dr. Mace. It seems Dr. Mace died two-months prior to our arrival. I guess someone forgot to keep tabs on his records. Thankfully, Ms. Emch and Mr. Macpherson made copies because after their discovery those records disappeared. I attribute the death record to human error. The students protest it wasn't. The social security number at hospital records was the same as the death certificate. I want my students off of this trail. I know where it leads. I insist that it must be human error and asked them what else they found.

They said Maria Rivera did not exist outside of hospital records. In fact, they couldn't even access her admittance into the hospital; no information about how she got there was available. The only information on Maria was her diagnosis and related symptoms, which we'd all seen. Hospitalized for two years seen by two doctors: Dr. Mace and Dr. Stewart. Stewart left the hospital almost a year ago and has been on hiatus since. Maria's entire background from hospital staff. She did not exist prior to her admittance. I change the subject.

"Do any of you have input about Mrs. Rivera's delusions?"

Mr. LaDay chuckles, "I believe her connection to family and science intersect, making her diagnosis for extreme symptoms exponentially more complicated. They overlap into other areas defined in other disease symptom groups."

"Come on Danny! Stop. This is a serious question." Ms. Thick protests.

"No, no, I'm serious."

"Absolutely ridiculous." She mumbles under her breath.

He continues, "Look, this lady came from somewhere. I will admit her delusions are a bit much. She thinks our dear Professor is her long lost husband who now has a completely different face. Yes, the lady is a bit off. Medications have only worsened her condition. I believe the proper treatment will be found to help fight her triggers. She doesn't see pink flying elephants or flying saucers. She only slightly warps her sense of reality. If we find what delusions trigger her symptoms I think we will better treat her condition."

Ms. Thick darts into the discussion.

"A secret race of super-humans traveling at light speed throughout the universe control this planet and have enslaved us to mine natural resources. The woman believes she is an alien. How is that only slightly warped? You can't be serious."

"Traci, how close-minded you are. You're a pretty girl; you should be a model or something. Why don't you leave the fancy stuff to serious scholars of behavioral science?"

"She thinks she's an alien!"

"You think you're a student of science!"

Mr. Macpherson referees to stop the back and forth.

"I think we need to focus on objective facts instead of subjective perspectives. We have a seriously ill patient who needs our help. We have some questionable activity which needs to be investigated. We can all agree on those facts. Now, are we going to come up with solutions, or are we going to abandon this case to name calling? If anyone wants to quit, then please let us know so those of us who want to proceed with the Professor can do so. I'm not here to find out who's the smartest, I'm here to complete this class and help this patient. I'm not sure if we are going to solve this woman's problems in one semester of study, but I do believe we can affect some positive changes in her situation."

"Hey, I'm with you," Mr. LaDay asserts, proclaiming his allegiance to the course, "I may not be right, but there's something we can do. That's all I was trying to say."

Ms. Thick moves in to underplay her previous contribution, "I'm just gonna leave, my opinion is worth nothing unless I just agree. It seems as if I'm disrupting the class."

Ms. Emch bolsters Ms. Thick, "Traci, don't leave. I'd like to hear what you have to propose. Please."

The reassuring Mr. Macpherson, "Yeah I want to hear what you have to say. Please, Traci. Let me know."

My turn to inject in the conversation.

"Ms. Thick, please share your thoughts on elevation of treatment. What do you suggest for our plan of action?"

She turns and looks around the class.

"We should wait, investigate and hear more. We don't need to have papers to tell us where she came from or why she's there. We don't need to find Dr. Stewart to learn what happened in his sessions. We have her own reflections of experiences."

Mr. LaDay, "I thought she was too crazy or too delusional to treat?"

"That's not what I was saying! I'm not saying we can't help her. I'm saying that her delusions are not realistic. We don't need to try to find truth in her delusions. We are supposed compile data to help her doctors bring her as close to reality as possible. We aren't supposed to merely believe her. We are supposed to study her and recommend possible treatments based on our studies."

"Are we supposed to bring her back then, Traci? Just pretend her delusions never happened?"

"No, Danny, but believing or feeding into her delusions is counterproductive. How are we going to help her if we continue doing what's making her sick?"

"Well then, do we treat her or give up and label treatment impossible? What do we do?"

"I just said it, Danny. We investigate and listen. We find out, deduce, where her delusional thinking is coming from. There is truth hidden in what she says, but only in her memories of experience, not fantasy. We need to shift the topic of conversation to her life and not why she believes in her delusions."

"Thank you, Ms. Thick. This will be the strategy for our next session. Are we all in agreement? If so, then class is dismissed. If not, then state your opposition in the same way as you did in this class on the first day."

Everyone looks to be in agreement as they begin to gather their things.

"We will meet and develop our questions and methods regarding implementation of Ms. Thick's strategy. Our next session with the patient will be in a week. See you all bright and early tomorrow. Your homework is to brainstorm. Enjoy your evening and have a good night."

Chapter VIII: My Princess

A morning sky blanketed by thick, dark clouds made it feel like evening more than morning. My mind is focused on a child I do not know. I see Maria today. A smile found my face as I embraced the wind and cold and I walked outside to my car. It was time for work. The sunrise of a man who enjoys his job.

Dr. Mace briefed us on Maria's status. My students and I developed our approach. We spent most of the week off campus devising plans and developing theories. We spent time at an appropriately named place called Willow's Park near my home. The scene was dotted with lush Willow trees with a rocky creek running around its perimeter. Koi ponds welcomed visitors at each of the two park entrances. Wood benches and stone pathways led to open grass areas with concrete picnic tables, fixed fountains and statutes gracing the park. No matter how many people are at Willow's Park, the sounds heard are mostly wind and crows. Sit comfortably anywhere to relax. The first day, my students and I stayed for almost four hours talking more about life in general than session outlines. It created a rewarding bond; an experience that left an impression. Ms. Thick and Mr. LaDay still bickered over most things. Mr. Macpherson, checked his watch frequently, seeming pressed for time. Ms. Amen was, as always, observant and quiet. Ms. Emch, however, piqued my interest.

On one occasion that week when I entered the park, I crossed paths a familiar curly haired woman on her way out of the park. At first, I couldn't place where I'd seen her before. I watched her walk a little after she passed me; she didn't look back. At the time, I didn't think much of it. Maybe I didn't know her. Maybe she just looked familiar. We broke for lunch that day and as usual I went to my car parked under one of the Willow trees. I was startled to see the curly haired woman and Ms. Emch talking in Ms. Emch's car. It looked to be a casual conversation, but then the woman struck Ms. Emch in the face. They continued talking, embraced, and then kissed, like the slap never happened. I felt voyeuristic as I watched. The curly-haired woman left the car and exited the park on foot. Ms. Emch fixed her hair and make-up before rejoining us after lunch. Her participation that afternoon showed no signs of emotional distress. Then it hit me, the curly haired woman had been at the class when I'd dismissed the final selection after their first assignment.

Maria's week had been surprisingly normal for someone in her condition. She participated actively in group activities, table games, T.V. time, and group conversations. Without sedatives, she'd managed many hours of sleep, only getting up for her routine pacing every three to four hours. Now I enter the room to begin the session we'd planned at Willows Park, Ms. Amen again by my side.

I wondered if she'd missed me. I'd soon have my answer.

"Good morning, Maria."

She looked at me with discontent then curiosity.

"Good morning, Adam. What kept you away so long?"

"I wasn't sure if you wanted to see me anymore."

"You weren't sure? Then, why are you here now?"

Pause.

"Because I had to see you. I missed you."

"You missed me?"

"Yes, I missed you a lot."

"Then why'd you stay away?"

"I just told you."

"No, you haven't told me anything."

"I'm not sure I follow what you mean?"

"You're not a good liar, Adam. What brings you here today?"

"I... I want to know about our child."

She looked away.

"What do you want to know?"

"Where is our child, Maria?"

"She's where you left me... and her."

"Her?"

"Yes her. You had a daughter."

"Had?"

She looked back at me.

"Yes, had! You no longer have one. You... never had one."

"Is she dead?"

"She might as well be. You will never see her. So it really doesn't matter."

"Yes it does. I want to see her."

"Well... that's not... that's not going to happen, Adam."

"Why?"

"Because she's gone. She'd dead to us."

"What do you mean?"

"She's gone, Adam! I don't know where she is. I don't know who she's with. I can't search for her and you're not going to know where to look."

"Maria, tell me what happened. I'll look anywhere."

"We'll see. Do you remember when I talked about how it is for the Originals' protection to keep us here, but the smallest Controllers figured out how to overcome it? Do you? It's because the smaller Controllers and largest Protectors are at odds with the Originals. The Originals live beyond this planet. The smallest and largest are their slaves too. Just Centurion shepherds. It's really very funny because for thousands of years on earth, the largest and smallest thought themselves to be allies with the Originals. The smallest largest and largest smallest have since rebelled. We now sit in the midst of rebellion."

"We sit in the midst?"

"Yes, Adam. In the midst of a war. The Originals have lost control of this planet. This is not a physical war, it's psychological. You see, the Originals travel thousands of human-years into the future within a matter of earth months; they are pure energy. This is proving to be a bit of a weakness because though the Controllers and Protectors each move slower in time travel they create more during time, thus effectively making them able to produce drastic changes in a matter of weeks like mold on fruit. The Controllers aren't always on earth. Only the Protectors are always on earth. Think about it, Adam. *Think about it.* How much do humans create in five years? The Originals travel at light speed, come back to a world full of changes.

We move very fast here on Earth. Remember, light speed is relative. Normals drink coffee because they're slaves. Exhausted from too much work building and sustaining the colony. We sell our time for money; we pay our Protectors, but they don't want money. They created money. They pay us money for our time of life. The Earth is your birth right. The Originals gave us everything we need. The Protectors charge us money for things that naturally exist. The money is a carrot on a stick to have us sell our time, we are tricked slaves. Drink coffee. Stay up. Work hard. Pay for the coffee. Coffee grows from the soil of earth. Coffee comes from Earth. Everything on Earth is yours. They charge you money for something which grows. Sell your time for money. You do what's demanded for a price. Still believe? Believe in the money. You need coffee, Adam? I hate being upset with you. I'm just so mad you lied. You see how fast we move?"

She turned to Ms. Amen standing beside me. The almost invisible deaf girl looked uneasy as Maria moved in her direction. A lioness locked on vision of prey. She moved behind the smaller woman, and sniffed her hair. She stopped abruptly to face me, displaying her prowess with pride.

"The energy transference: death and birth is a cycle of life that holds us captive. These prisons our spirit bodies. It is what they use against us. Energy is formless – it is creation. The Originals are formless. We are one with all. We are all a part of the same energy. Our physical bodies' individual forms separating us to create time and place. The time you have between birth and death. How long is your life? The place of impressions accumulated observations of reflection is where you become the ego you think you are. Time and place create the form. No two individuals can occupy the same time and place. So, I can't stand where this little bitch is standing as she's standing there. We were born at different moments, in different places of occupied space. It's what makes us all unique. Yet we are all essentially the same being of spirit. Trillions of different moments to equal observed experience. We hold our space in time equal to our differences – but

64

don't confuse separation and individuality, we are always seeking to come together. Sex, our energy together. Male and female anatomy, merges energy to give birth to new forms of life."

She sniffs Ms. Amen. Without warning, snatching the young girl by her shirt and raising her off her feet. The shocking scene freezes me in place. My mind translating thoughts with no physical action.

"See, Adam! No matter where I put this bitch, I can never be in her position. I can never be where this bitch is standing. Always next to you. Always with you. I have to go a week from you if I make you mad baby!"

Several bulky staff members come to restrain her. She releases Ms. Amen as the staff try to sedate her.

"I was good all week. I knew you'd be watching me. I knew if I was good enough, you'd come back. Why can't I be her?! Why can't I be her?!"

I ask Dr. Mace not to sedate her too heavily. I wanted to continue the session. The audio recording replaying in my mind stopped with Maria's screaming.

Ms. Amen, though visibly shaken, was not injured. Dr. Mace recommends Ms. Amen not return with me to the session; the students and I agree. We did not factor Ms. Amen's presence being perceived as a threat, or stimulating jealousy. We did not factor the effect my absence would have on her behavior. By allowing her to express more delusion than reality I failed my students. I have to re-evaluate my actions. My students urge me to continue my approach her as her husband. I asked Dr. Mace if I could be waiting for Maria when she came back to the observation room. He agrees.

Standing in the room for the first time by myself, I try to imagine what my wife feels in this room. Is she afraid? Is she nervous? How might she be feeling?

The door slides open quietly. Beautiful, she stands half-clothed in her hospital gown, her hair wet from perspiration. She shivers a little as she enters the room. The door closes behind her. Her eyes are cast down, the visible shame from her earlier outburst. She stares at the floor waiting to be scolded.

"Maria."

She jumps a little but continues looking at the ground.

"Maria."

Nothing.

"Maria, I'm sorry for being away from you so long. I want you to know... that woman means nothing to us. You are all that's important to me and I'm going to prove that to you every minute of my life."

She looks at me. Her beautiful green eyes shining.

"Adam, do you still love me?"

I had to tell her, no matter how inappropriate.

"Yes, Maria. Yes, I still love you. I have never stopped loving you. All of this time, my thoughts have been with you. I died when I left you. I did everything in my power to block you out of my mind, but I could not. I felt as if a piece of me was missing; for years I felt incomplete. In my dreams, we dance together or sit in stillness observing the surroundings. For a brief moment when I wake I see you lying next to me, only to find it's just a shadow of you as I open my eyes. I miss you."

She reaches out and touches my lips.

"Shhh...."

She moves her index finger from my mouth and catches one of the tears rolling down my cheek. She stares at the tear she captured, studying it. She holds that finger out. Her eyes soften. She brings the tear to her lips and kisses it.

"Our daughter's name is Nancy."

"Nancy?"

"Yes, Adam, Nancy. She is quite beautiful. She has your eyes."

"Where is she, Maria? I want to see her."

"I told you, Adam; you will not be able to do that."

"Why?"

"Because she's gone."

"Is she still alive?"

"I don't know. They took her."

"Who? Who took her?"

"Adam... Do you know why it's hard to see deformity or abnormality in human beings?"

I swallow my desire to know what happened to our daughter. I didn't want to upset her again.

"No Maria, why?"

"Because we're all the same of spirit. You don't want to identify with others' deformity, so you feel apprehensive when you see it because you sense the possibility of your own abnormalities. The way we see the differences in others is a reflection of how we see ourselves. Evil exploits our differences. They make us fight each other over foolish imaginations. The wars distract the slaves. Humans naturally wish to conquer each other. It's another way to manage our thoughts and keep the focus off of the truth. The Originals never intended to interfere with this process. This process creates a natural balance of energy."

"A natural balance of energy?" I play the game.

"Yes, Adam. The natural balance of energy: population control. Evil unnaturally controls human population to fit their timelines of technological innovation. If we multiply too fast, we lose other species and duplicate. In the billions of combinations DNA can have almost perfect replications. There are only 9 billion configurations of DNA before human double helix duplicates or mutates to another species of human. You know that from science class. One species flourishes and another goes extinct. Energy has to be drawn from somewhere. Since we have no natural predators, we are forced to balance ourselves. What would our population be without medicine and hospitals? We have no season for mating. We multiply so fast. All of our wars, diseases, and murderers don't even put a dent in our growth. The evil exploit our similarities and create imaginary differences. The Controllers command us to do so."

"Imaginary differences?"

She laughed at me.

"Keep up, Adam. We're on stage right now. Smile for the camera... The imaginary differences are things we create. Religion for example; two groups believe in God, yet they worship differently – war.

Competition, another imaginary difference. Competition a measure of time. Time is a creation. The calculation of time is not natural. It is a means to confuse you and disconnect you from true life. You lose touch with the solstices and lunar cycles, and you watch a clock and calendar. Given the same conditions and standards, we can all do the same thing. We just need time to prepare. Selfishness is the inability to share, it's also the root of our survival skills: survival of the fittest, self-preservation. So, is selfishness bad? Confusion... Confusion... Adam, you guide me. You are now exploiting my natural instincts with illusions from other people's suggestions, but I still love you. All of this stuff around us is from other people's minds. This is not real between us. These are illusions! This wall, this floor, these clothes. Illusions."

She bangs her fist on the wall,

"Illusions...Illusions...Illusions."

I grab her, she screams. She squirms. Her energy is focused on me -- her lips, her tone, the softness of her touch arouses. I want to fuck her right here. I want to raise her hospital gown and insert myself. Happy that she feels me become harder, she grabs my manhood with a firm but soothing grip. She squeezes me. I have to pull her away. I can't catch my breath to form words. My heartbeat pounds from my chest to stomach. Chills erupt on my skin. I feel as if I'm going to climax. Her voice finishes the job. A visibly shocking jolt. She walks back to the door.

"I miss how you taste in my mouth, baby. Mmmm... I love you. Diversion is their best tool. The media diverts our attention helping you lose focus. Each news story gives us something to think about. If we focus on the topics they create, what time do we have for ourselves? Topics brought to us give us directives, options. So many to choose from. *Do you believe in this? We need to fight for that. How could they do this? Who did that? Trust this study. Trust that study. This person did this today. This is what they're doing to us.*

"Impulse information that dulls our thinking. The Controllers construct and define what beauty is by constantly showing us symbols of what they want beauty to be: the sexiest man alive, models, actresses, actors. The moment we are born images are chosen for us by those who control the information we see and hear. The Controllers give us dreams and illusions to chase. They tell us how to keep up with our Joneses.

"The people who first encountered television believed it to be a tool of the devil. Were they right? Well it depends on what your interpretation of the devil is. Nevertheless, those people who lived before television realized a Beast was entering their home. This monster establishing itself as the main orator of the family unit. It went from a cooperative family and community group relationship to a personal, private, individualistic relationship. We all have self-preservation instincts that drive us to make all sorts of decisions. The media monster dominates most of our homes, influencing most of our decisions. The energy of trending popular culture. They are filling our heads with the information they want us to receive. Is it entertainment or is it the numbing effect of mind control? Media. Millions upon millions of minds opened to the airwaves, connected to the television program. It is what it says it is: a program. All of these minds connected and stimulated by impulses which they tweak and effect with commercials, news, public announcements, and featured broadcasts. Broadcast what? Hmmmm... I know! Broadcast a spell. The program tailored to give you ideologies, introduce you to horrific things, desensitize you and expose you to new ideas. It is the intrusion of a Beast that programs your mind with impulse stimulation. Think about how you'd feel if you'd never seen a car or airplane, then suddenly one appeared before you. You'd be awestruck with a lack of understanding as to what you were seeing. These things are normal to us because we see them all the time. Think about how many things television, radio and internet programming exposes you to that which you have not seen before. It is the work of a Beast, a Beast which we are all part of. We work to feed it as it grows bigger and stronger from our labors. What are cities without workers? We are the blood that flows through the cities' veins. We build it bigger and stronger. As we expand, it expands. You see, my love, the only problem we have is that the ones who control us are thousands of years older. We move fast. Our works come at the speed of light. You can see how truly

69

remarkable we are when viewing time lapse photography. You blink a universal eye and a planet circles the sun a hundred times and horse driven buggies are replaced by muscle cars. The Originals are aliens from the previous planet and only mere moments of their life pass. Imagine how they must see us; one hundred rotations to us is only a few weeks of their travels. We aren't watched through our perception of time. We are watched at light speed in flashes of time lapse. I want to see that girl again."

"Why... Why do you want to see her?"

"Because I remember her face. She's not one of us. Stay away from her."

" She's not one of us?"

" No... She's one of them. She's a Controller. She's here for suppression."

"No. She's okay."

"No. She's not! Stay away from her."

"Why Maria?"

"Why do you question me? Do you love her, Adam?"

"No! I don't love her."

"I am your wife, Adam."

"I know. I know who you are, Maria."

She walks to me from the door, her look now one of seductive innocence. Once in range, she kisses my cheek.

"Trust me, Adam. I am your wife. Promise me you won't talk to her anymore. Promise me."

"I promise, my love." I lie.

She kisses my cheek again, smiling playfully.

"You did that without hesitation. I like that. It's a good sign of loyalty. Stay loyal to me, Adam."

"I will my love. Look at me."

The silence on the recording runs a little over a minute. I lost myself in her as the deepest parts of our higher selves connected though eye contact.

"I will always be loyal to you. I will always remain by your side. I pledge my life to you, Maria. Do you hear me?"

"Yes... Yes I hear you."

"I love you, Maria."

"I love you too. I'm tired. I need to go to bed."

"Okay"

"Will you come see me again soon?"

"Yes. I will be here tomorrow."

She jumps up and kisses me.

"I knew you loved me! I knew you loved me!"

"Yes, I do."

I stop the recording.

Chapter IX: Goodbye

Dr. Mace carries a briefcase to his car. Dusk in the hospital parking lot. Our conversation after Maria's fourth session leads me to believe Dr. Mace is one of them. The stout, bald man waddles as he walks across the large parking lot. I sit in my car with an overwhelming desire to run him down. I wanted to know what he did to Maria.

He says he distrusts my methods. He questions my conduct, accusing me of a lack of ethics and professionalism. He proclaims he can see where my charade is leading from my actions demonstrating a desire to violate her. Kissing a patient is unprofessional under any circumstances and we kissed, or I allowed her to kiss me. As a doctor I crossed serious boundaries. Her reaction to our touch; my reaction to our touch. My wife. He wants me to stop touching her. They want to torture me. All I can do is agree. I watch him drive away, as I follow cautiously.

I have always prided myself for staying out of situations that can cause me embarrassment. For example, I never gamble because I don't like to lose. Remaining a winner establishes an air of superiority over those around you. I don't allow people to see me lose. Embarrassment means I'm exposed, exposure means vulnerability; I pride myself on staying away from situations that cause me embarrassment. Tonight I abandon my inhibitions and find myself in a situation of vulnerability. I recognize my weakness: love.

We arrive at the place where Dr. Mace enjoys his evenings. It's a lovely residence with a modest view of the town lights. A home that looks comfortable in its surroundings. Trees conceal its full scope and insulate it into seclusion.

Parked a few houses away, ducking low in my car, I watch him go inside. The street is quiet. I get out of my car and make my way down the quiet street assuming an appearance of a regular evening stroll. My nerves and gut tingle in tandem with my steps. Dr. Mace's home, the finish-line of my journey. I hide amongst the trees to study his environment, his life, him. I look for something, anything, to explain what he'd done, what he continues to do.

He sits in his study online perusing media information and communication. I move in the shadows of his property searching for signs of a family. As far as I can tell, he lives alone. His home is quiet and still with no sign of children; no toys, balls or video games. Also absent is the soft, warm signs of a woman's touch: no flowers or vases, no extra pillows on the couches. A place set for one at the kitchen table; a half-drunk bottle of wine sits next to a single glass, a half-finished plate of food: the meal of a lonely man. He'd eaten his meal and retired to his study.

Under the cover of pine trees between his and his neighbor's homes, I move in the shadows. A dark car drifts down the street coming to rest in front of the house. I take cover behind pine bark. A woman on the phone and a small child emerge from the vehicle. The woman is finishing her phone conversation as she and the girl make their way to Dr. Mace's home. The car rolls away as stealthily as it arrived. As they approach the front steps Dr. Mace opens the door seeming anxious to usher them inside. I move to another viewpoint so I can watch their interaction. Dr. Mace tends to the girl. Hanging her coat in the hall closet, then fixing her a sandwich and a glass of juice. While the little girl eats, he and the woman speak with a tone connoting a serious conversation. I can't hear what they are saying, but Dr. Mace is upset. At one point, he grabs the woman firmly by her shoulders in an effort to emphasize his words. The woman nods in agreement. The two separate and he returns to the little girl while the woman makes a phone call.

After finishing her call the woman returns to the kitchen. The three interact without affection, no smiles, no joy. They treat the little girl as like they are her caretakers. When the child finishes her meal, they put her in a bedroom that is clearly not hers. There are no dolls, no toys, no affects to resemble a little girl's room. They put her there with no hug or kiss goodnight.

Dr. Mace and the woman talk briefly before the same black car reappears on the street. The woman answers her phone and quickly hangs up. Dr. Mace escorts her to the door. Once the woman leaves he returns to his study, pausing in moments of reflection until he falls asleep. It is all like a dream to me. I think I've just seen my daughter for the first time.

The next day I meet my students in the parking lot of the hospital. I am exhausted. Even with my fatigue I notice Ms. Emch fidgeting with her hands. Why is she nervous? I make a mental note to learn more. With everyone together we go inside.

This session will include Mr. LaDay. He accompanies me as a colleague. I feel a male presence might be less threatening. She will be less inclined to molest me. A new element to the aura of the session Mr. LaDay. His energy a silent challenge I can utilize to gain more control of the interview's tone and direction.

Ms. Amen hands me a small, folded piece of paper. Her subtlety makes the exchange almost anonymous. The piece of paper seems to press in my palm from thin air. She doesn't stop me or slow me down. She moves past me only briefly catching my eye. I glance at the paper, *Read alone* written on the front. I catch her eye once more but she looks away.

Dr. Mace greets us in the observation room. I feel a stronger connection to him. He doesn't look the same to me. The sterility imbued by his position has lost its severity; he is now simply a man in a coat doing his job.

I inform him of my plan to include Mr. LaDay in the session. No objection. We are briefed on Maria's behavior and condition. She has been allowed only a sleep medication, which did little to stop her nightly ritual of pacing the floor. She's behaving cordially with the staff. Dr. Mace applauds her behavior and attributes her change to our work.

In the observation room she sits patiently. The door opens. Her eyes light up when she sees me. She stands to greet me. Mr. LaDay enters her eyes change, becoming cold and angry.

"Who is he? Why is he here?" She demands.

I motion to Mr. LaDay stop moving.

"Maria. He's with me. He's good."

"No! No he's not. He's one of them. Look in his eyes. Look at him. Look how he looks at me."

I look at Mr. LaDay, who appears calm.

"Maria... your response. He's not one of them. He has no idea what we're talking about."

Inquisitively, trying to sense him through her gaze, she stares. Narrowing her eyes and tilting her head, through an eerie silence she stops and smiles.

"People's eyes see their world. Everyone lives with a different perspective of the moment. All of our perspectives live in a unique time and space. Here, right now we are all together. Yet we all have different views of this same situation. See? Ha, ha... I said 'see'... Get it? Anyway, we view different reflections at opposite angles at the same time. You're looking at me while I'm looking at you. I'm your reflection. You are my reflection. We see each other and in seeing each other, we see ourselves. You are me and I am you. The only thing which separates us is time and space; this gives us perspective, our experience and understanding."

She turns her back to us and stares at the observation camera. I motion for Mr. LaDay to enter the room. The door closes behind him. She runs toward us with an object in her hand. I catch her. She screams.

"His eyes have seen it! You can't hide it from me. I know what the truth looks like. He's one of them! He's one of them!"

The hospital staff rush in to subdue her. The object in my hand. Why did she have a weapon? Was it meant for me? It is the top of a can; my hand is cut. What just happened? Why did she react so strangely?

"Do you hear me, Professor? How did she know what?"

Dr. Mace asks. Listening to the recording now, I don't remember saying what's recorded.

"How did she know Mr. LaDay would be here today?"

"She didn't know, Professor. How could she know? I didn't even know. I'm the one who escorted you from the observation room and you were with me the entire time. Ms. Rivera obviously intended to harm you or whoever else walked into the room. I'm sorry, Professor. Your access to Ms. Rivera is now prohibited pending a full evaluation by our staff and our board. Your contact with staff here is also suspended. I have to tend to my patient. Please excuse me."

"Doctor, please let me see her once more. You can't stop it now. We are on the verge of a breakthrough."

"I can and I have stopped it. Have my staff look at your hand on the way out. If you have any problems with my decision, take it up with the board. This conversation is over. Good day, Professor."

"Doctor..."

He is gone.

Chapter X: Mistress

It is cold and the rain falls hard day and night. At times when hail beats against my window I hear the sounds of a crazed mob fighting to break barriers that deny them entrance. Again I am without her. My class is on winter break. When I venture out into the darkness to see a student ice batters my body as I run from my house to my car.

The curly haired woman has me curious, or should I say concerned. I've seen people struck before, but not that viciously only to still seem unfazed by it. Ms. Emch returned to our study group that day in somewhat of a trance. I wanted to know what that was about.

We meet at a campus exhibit: the history of civilization. Cro-Magnon, Neolithic, Iron Age, Ice Age, computer age, et cetera. His story.

She is dressed in black knee-high stiletto boots over dark, form fitting jeans, and a green cashmere sweater. Her hair, nails, and make up are all manicured to perfection. She is stunning.

We walk and talked about the exhibit and life in general. I pick her brain, analyzing her thoughts but barely sharing myself in return.

Newly single, she tells me her divorce had recently been finalized. She looks forward to a renewed, independent life. This I learn in response to a comment from me,

"I'm sure your companion is very pleased with your educational productivity."

She takes me into her world, telling me she doesn't have a companion and she isn't interested in dating anyone. Off my tongue,

"I find it shocking you don't have any suitors. There should be a line of men waiting to court you assiduously."

She smiles graciously and bats her eyelashes as her cheeks become flush.

"Not having a companion doesn't mean I don't have suitors."

There is a hint of something I can't quite place in her voice. This night I'm lost in a soul's dying wish to be free of form. I'd do everything in my power to pursue the physical rewards of her releasing my spirit from form. An archangel in high heeled boots delivers me.

Drinking eases my ability to face life without her after losing her a second time. I love the way the strong poison numbs my body from my mind. I escape from the prison of reality. The hospital board's investigation of our sessions with Maria will take longer than the remainder of the academic year. It might be a full year before I know the decision of if... she is gone for real. My only friend the Dean, tells me to find another subject to study the coming semester; the school board is trying to pull the University out of this particular case. In their eyes it is done. Over. Reality. Take a sip. I have to sort through a list of cases and find a new subject. I see the files of potential case studies piled in my living room. Thirty or forty, I think. I still have not moved. Another sip. Okay. Sort through the stack and submit five potential candidates to the Dean after the holiday break. I can handle that. All I have to do is touch one. The stack sits there watching me numb myself to the world, drinking poison. My body and mind finally separate.

Am I a functioning alcoholic, or just a drunk? I walk and talk. I don't shower or bathe properly. I slur when I speak and stagger when I walk. I know I'm a complete mess, but I can't bring myself to care. I'm okay as long as I don't. That's how I live among the public, numb, asleep.

My inbox is full of emails. I've just woken from passing out earlier in the evening. It is late at night and the rain is pelting against the window. My house is freezing, my heart is pounding. Still drunk, I decide to see if I still have a job. I scan my emails to see what the world wants from me; the only thing I could probably accomplish before getting another bottle and drink to pass out again.

Scanning through junk emails I view a strange message.

Your two-hour session tonight with Violet at The Cave is been confirmed. Bring a pair of stockings and high heel shoes in your size. She'll see you at 10pm. Do not make Her angry. Be on time.

- Violet

78

The picture at the bottom of the page resembles Ms. Emch. My lust teased loins stir vigorously. Viewing the temptation of a provocative experience I find another bottle and stare at her picture repeating the message until I pass out. When I wake she looks different. Still her. The picture was now staring at me with stern disapproval. I click a link the email and am directed to *The Cave*, a private dungeon. Entering the site I search for Violet and find my Mistress.

Her beauty is more than I can take in with a solitary glance. I get lost in the details of several photos... Very stimulating photos. I can't turn away in fear that I miss anything of her. Her profile states: *There is no limit to fantasy and the only limit to pain is the mind. I will free your spirit from your body.*

She takes my breath away. In the course of our interaction, I created an idea of what I believed her life to be. She exudes a quiet confidence, commanding attention. How many times do we say, "I should've known," or "Why didn't I see that coming?" Getting caught up in our own daily activity, very seldom do we pay attention to the people around us. We don't notice things that in hindsight we feel we should have noticed. She is only my imagination and I want more. My full attention is consumed by motivation from a primal hunger to satisfy a new beautiful obsession. From my mind I'm doled a sober experience.

I call Ms. Emch and Ms. Amen and ask them to help me review the possible case studies. They both agree to come. Our date is set in motion. We review the files at my home, changing the elements of our personal interaction to one that is more familiar.

She arrives first. I find it hard not to stare. Her commanding attention to the details of her appearance were more my reason for staring than her physical attributes. The private knowledge of a surreptitious life adds a lot to the eyes curiosity. Before me stands a woman with a secret life, unaware I know her reticence for revelation.

A fitted white blouse, black pants... the same black stiletto boots from our night at the exhibit. I take her jacket savoring it before I hang it in the closet; she smells of vanilla and sandalwood. The flavorful scent fills my nostrils supplying me with a tasteful reminding of her presence. I return from hanging her coat intoxicated with euphoria to find her admiring the mask above the fireplace. My favorite affect. How does she know? The African death mask Eshu, used by ancient priests during human sacrifice. She touches it. Then says,

"Why choose an ancient sign of death to hang so prominently in your living room?"

I explain, "The priests who used this mask believed in their intentions. These priests believe that by taking the lives of those who did not want to die, that God would be pleased. They believed they were doing right when they wore this mask. Today some look on their actions as atrocious or barbaric, as future generations may look at us in our times by our actions. Whatever the case, human intentions are based on beliefs. We send young men and women to fight and die in wars. Our intentions for sending them, we believe, may be good, just as those priests who wore the mask believed their intentions to be good. The mask represents human beliefs and is a reminder to myself to be aware of my own intentions, my human intentions."

When I listen to the audio I recorded for that day, I'm always curious about what she thought during the silence following my explanation. A long silence of almost two minutes. I still feel tortured when I hear it.

She just stares at the mask, not breaking her gaze for one moment. The silence is interrupted by a knocking on the door. She turns to me smiling, I smile back, then answer the door.

The day slipped into evening as we all sorted through the files. Ms. Amen found an interesting case of an old judge who believed a secret master race of humans was controlling the world. He believed this secret group of people were out to destroy him because of what he knows. His delusions caught our interest, as did his age. 115 years old. He's complained on more than one occasion of feeling as if his skin were on fire, and that he was trapped inside a prison called human existence. We agreed this case could set a precedent for delusional similarities in patients with common forms of mental illness. We would find a common thread that triggers this type of behavior. We found our next case study, Mr. Clark a.k.a. "Bug". The only submission I'd offer the Dean.

We enjoy the rest of our evening over wine and pizza. I play back the audio recording. Ms. Amen's participation in the discussion. She speaks not one word, only sometimes laughing. Nothing else. Her laugh is out of tune, at times out of place, always inappropriate. We laugh with her for politeness. When they leave, I spend more time studying sadomasochism. I find myself going deeper in search of salvation; a moment to be free from the torturous wonderings of my love and how she could be. Was she warm in this cold weather? Was she sleeping well? Does she feel me missing her? Some thoughts take the air I breathe. God I need air. I'm suffocating. Only a harsh echoing taunts as answer to my questions.

Consumed within a world of dominate or be dominated. Sacrificing for forgiveness. Tantalizing. Perverse thoughts. I find a private dungeon called *The Offering*. I see no one who looks familiar. This taboo, this secret, my diversion to physical pain to quell my mental anguish. A hidden world where the thoughts of my mind can be separated from my body. A place where my deviant spirit will be accepted with open arms.

It is a numb burn that separates flesh from the spirit. Tied to an apparatus called the horse I am standing, bent to 90 degrees, my wrists are bound to it, anchoring me in my position. My backside a focus of concentration for her disposition of judgment. Mistress agreed to the role of Maria. Her long, single tail whip laps at my skin, scolding me for loving Her. Generously She allowed me to record the audio of my offering.

"Apologize for what you have done. Look at you. You disgust me. You lie to me? You leave me?"

She strikes me hard on my thighs. No part of my body can be spared in the release of my essence from form. I am allowed no covering to protect myself from Her implements. She instructs me to lift one foot behind me. The flesh I stand on is yet untouched. With a thin rattan cane she strikes the bottom of my foot. The sharp burn of the cane turns my flesh into warm pads; I am hovering above myself.

"Repeat after Me: 'I will not be selfish thinking only of my needs. I will honor the needs and desires of Mistress above my own.'"

Hard across my back a braided, leather flogger falls. A gunshot sound on the recording. *Whack! Whack!*

She commands, "Repeat my words!"

My own scream is unrecognizable. Her voice echoes around the room before reaching into my comprehension. I tried to speak but nothing came out. How could I repeat Her words without my voice? A sonorous pain brings me back to the body of my circumstance.

"I... I... I will nnnaaauhtra ... aht ..."

Whack! Her cane across my ass. The sharp penalty radiated from its point of impact.

"I CAN'T HEAR YOU!"

Whack!

The anger inside me awakens. My scream morphs to a growl. I strain flexing my muscles against leather restraints. My voice through gritted teeth. I have a feeling that could lift a thousand pounds.

"I WILL NOT BE SELFISH!"

Whack!

Whack!

"I CAN'T HEAR YOU!" She screams.

Whack!

My body flexes with an unfelt power and I dig my nails deep into my palms breaking flesh.

"I WILL NOT BE SELFISH! I WILL HONOR THE NEEDS AND DESIRES OF MY MISTRESS, AND MY MISTRESS ONLY!"

Whack!

The cane slaps my calves, my legs buckle. My essence returns to form. Her palm, soft and soothing caresses my back, the bites of Her cane replaced, the reward for doing as I am told. A shadowy figure unties my hands and I'm free from the clutches of the horse. I collapse.

"Crawl to me." She purrs.

The lighter tips of Her flogger kiss my tender ass. Her purr transforms to a growl.

"Kiss my feet, you worthless piece of garbage. Submit."

I crawl in pain, focused on reaching her boots. My body numb, the gift of welts covering me. Muscles sore from straining and flexing. I slow and flinch in the anticipation of another strike from Her powerful wishes. I fear what is connected to those boots. She murmurs softly.

"Untie my left boot and take it off. Kiss it first, kiss my boot."

I kiss it.

"Do you love it?" She inquires with a lilt in her voice.

"Yes, Mistress."

I pull myself up to stand on my knees. I bow before Her and untie Her boot.

"Don't ever leave me again. You belong to Me."

"Yes, Mistress."

"Kiss the bottoms of my feet."

"Yes, Mistress."

"Lick them."

"Yes, Mistress."

"Suck my toes."

"Yes, Mistress."

The salty taste of Her feet turns sweet in my mouth. Her approval. She allows me to suck the world from beneath her feet. It soothes me. She is the representation of the Beast. The Masters who control humanity strike us and beat us into submission and conformity, then allow us to suckle the dirt and sweat from their feet.

"Wipe my foot with your shirt."

She sounds upset.

In aching pain I retrieve the article of clothing requested, and with even more painful effort I return. Before Her on bended knees, I clean my saliva from Her feet.

"That is good. Place My boot back on My foot and state your pledge to Me."

Placing the boot back on Her foot, deliberately slowly I re-lace it.

"I will not be selfish. I will obey and honor my Mistress. I will not be selfish. I will obey and honor my Mistress."

I repeat until my task is complete. The ball of Her boot to my chest knocks me to the floor. Her final act of domination.

"Put your clothes back on and leave. You're dismissed."

"Yes, Mistress."

She slams the door behind Her.

I clothe myself crying quietly. I miss Her. The recording stops as I whisper, "I love you."

At home, I awake on the floor I feel like I've been drinking. I remember the experience of the night before in a fog. My computer has the audio file from my session with Mistress. I play the recording and I climax while listening. She sounds like my love. Almost identical. It stimulates me to take Her punishment. I associate it as a tribute to my love. Hours evaporate as I replay my favorite points of the recording. I can't pull myself away. I try to move with no physical attempts.

I am rescued by technology. An email. A message marked urgent from my assistant. Curious for distraction. I open it.

Dear Professor,

A recent death in my family requires me to return home to my native country. I do not know when I will return. I regret to inform you this message marks my notice of resignation. I deeply regret this untimely departure and this abrupt notice. I'm sending all of the documents regarding the class to your home address via registered mail. I am enclosing my access codes for my computer files along with the telephone number you can use to reach me for emergency purposes.

It has been a pleasure to work with you, sir and it is an honor to have known you. I trust we will keep in contact and talk in the future. Thank you very much.

Sincerely,

Mkeba

The message awakened my anxiety. My assistant my connection, my anchor. Brought to me by the Dean she is part of the underground.

Behind the scenes she has been enormously helpful in keeping me focused.

I reply thanking her for her valued service, extending my regards and condolences to her and her family. I have no assistant now.

In the bathroom I shower, shave, and think. I peel from my shirt from the wounds on my back. Raw and welted skin burns under the heat of the water. I find the perfect temperature to scald my naked body. I wince as the new water hits me and I force myself to endure and accept the pain. It becomes soothing and starts to arouse me. The downpour washes away my tears. Maria. I climax, thinking about her inflicting this pain on me. I deserve the punishment. I abandoned her again. In a corner of the bathtub, I curl my knees in my chest and my arms reach toward opposite fingers to lock around my shins. The searing liquid rains down upon me. I'm nowhere to be found – a missing person who looks familiar to those around him. The identity of my spirit is not the image I reflect. A false reflection, a relic commemorating I'm not who I want to be.

Impressions flash behind my eyelids: our wedding day, the first day I laid eyes on her, our first date, the first time we'd made love, a trip to the mountains camping under the stars, our ballooning trip -- that's how she talked me into skydiving. I told her I would, but only if we jumped together. She laughed at me and said, "How else were we going to do it?" Her beautiful smile... I see so clearly. We jumped out of a plane. I wasn't afraid. We were together and that's all that ever mattered. I knew in that moment of falling thousands of feet, holding her hand, that nothing was better than this. As long as I was with her everything would be fine. We flew that day, and then, I left her. I left her alone with the life we created surrounded by the people who wished to take that life from us. How could that equal a good intention? Regardless of the condition I was in, nothing should have been more important than being together. I told myself I was protecting her; saving her from people who wished to do us harm. I told myself over and over again all that mattered was her; but the truth is I should have died protecting her. I called myself smart. I knew the answer to my problem, her, and yet I created and lived through years of stupidity without her. She suffered because of my actions. We are apart. No amount of physical punishment compares to the suffering she endured. The welts on my back, the swelling, the humiliation multiplied a thousand times would barely measure the pain of our hearts. She loved me so much that she could see past my cosmetic surgery into my spirit and knew beyond a doubt it was me. I rise from the corner of the shower and open my eyes.

In a mad daze, I smash every bottle in the house. The spot from which I'd risen, now covered in jagged fragments. Glass shatters and bounces, a glistening array highlighting my failings. I refuse to feel the shards driving into my bare feet. I scream at the weakness inside me wishing to destroy it. Every shatter, a blow to my opposition, until I am left with no more to destroy. I collapse. Glass embedded in my hands, knees, soles. Blood flows to a glossy, crimson pool over the world beneath me. My physical limitations stain my place in time.

Tap...Tap... In the distance of my reality.

Tap...Tap... Is it the front door? I hear rattles of creaking wood after the strikes. *Tap...* Wind blowing hard outside. Trees whistling. *Bang...* A storm is here. Thunder after lightning. *Bam... Bam... Bam...* In semi-consciousness drawing a breath is labored action; the loss of blood in concert with fatigue. My eyes close a blink. They open and I am no longer in the bathroom. A shadow towers over me, my shoulders pinned down. A smaller figure rushes past the dark pillar above me, pinching me. They've captured me. Consciousness of form dissipates.

Maria's touching me holding my face, her hands are soft. I haven't felt comfort and security in years. I lean in to kiss her, to tell her I love her. She pulls away shaking her head. I struggle to understand why. It isn't her face. It isn't Maria...? Ms. Amen? A light takes her away. Unconscious, abstract thoughts connect to conscious reality.

From my bed I witness the morning sun push through the clouds. What happened? I'm in bed? Ms. Amen is staring at me, smiling. How did she get here? I ask questions, hoping for different answers than what's clearly apparent.

"Did you see the broken bottles in the bathroom?"

She nods.

"Did you get me into bed?"

She nods.

She stands 5'2" and weighs maybe 110 pounds. I'm almost a foot taller than her, and outweigh her by more than 100 pounds.

"Who helped you get me into bed?"

She smiles, turns, and walks out of the room.

Puzzled by her actions I lay in contemplation. My question unanswered —purposely? Someone had helped her. She returned with bacon, eggs, toast, sausage, and orange juice on a tray. I sat up smiling. She set the tray in front of me.

"Did you make this?"

She nods yes, smiles, and leaves the room.

I take a few bites. I can't taste it. Something smells sanitized. What is she cleaning? I pull myself from bed. My mind is still foggy; the pinch must have been a sedative. My sore feet, tender throbbing hands, and aching knees join forces to impair my mobility. This requires a great deal of concentration. I catch her in my sight and call out, forgetting she can't hear me, but surprisingly she turns around.

"How did you get me into bed? Who helped you?"

She smiles and points at me.

"I helped you?"

She nods.

How do I not remember helping myself into bed? I hadn't been drinking. I should remember what happened. Why would she lie? Frustration spurs swift anger. The words erupt from deep within me,

"Get out!"

She smiles.

"Get out!" I scream

Forgetting my cuts and wounds, ignited in a rage fueled by lack of understanding I march to the front door. I want her gone. I open the door forcefully, staring at her in disgust. She tilts her head and walks toward me without her smile. Looking into my eyes she passes the threshold, and whispers,

"I'm sorry."

I slam the door and close my eyes, savoring a few seconds of relief. I look outside. She is gone.

Deaf, with so much innocence in her eyes *she lied to me*? I remember something: the note she placed in my hand right before our last session.

A few weeks had passed, I couldn't remember where I placed it. I hadn't washed my clothes, or cleaned anything else since the last session with Maria. Thankful for piles of dirty laundry scattered everywhere, the haystacks for my needle. I don't remember what I wore that day. Pairs of slacks and jeans contain nothing I want. Business notes, money, a stick of gum, lint, and a pencil eraser are the rewards of my treasure hunt. I go through the pockets of each pair of pants three, four, five times. No note. Why hadn't I remembered sooner? I couldn't just turn around and ask her what the note contained, or could I? Would she reveal the true contents of the note? Did it matter? I want to know what it says. Yes, it matters; a mystery that could evade revelation matters. Without saying words she'd gotten to me. I need another appointment. I email Mistress. She's been waiting for me.

I'm blinded and bound to the St. Andrew's cross with my back to Mistress. My long sought release from the troubles of the day. She shows me no mercy. The wounds on my back reopen. St. Andrew, a man crucified for his wrongdoings. I deserve crucifixion. I need to be crucified, just like him. She whips me until I no longer scream. My back, my ass, my thighs, my calves, my arms receive no compassion. In a voice that mimics Maria's, She tells me to apologize for being worthless. She beats the words out of my mouth and I barely utter a sound. On the recording I cry as She calls me, *Dirt! Trash! Slime! Filth!* not even fit to lick the ground beneath Her feet. I just want Her approval. She unties me. Gravity pulls me to the floor. I lay in the fetal position.

"Lay on your stomach! You're a piece of dirt."

I do. My lips touch the floor. She walks toward me. I smell the leather of Her shoes approach before she shoves her toe under my ribs, kicking to turn me on my back.

"Lick the bottom of my boot."

Sandy specks of unknown particles crunch in my mouth as I clean. Satisfied, she slides the sole across my face, smearing the grimy wetness from my lips to my nose and cheek. I lay still wondering if She is done. Maybe She'll allow me to lick Her bare feet again. I hear fabric moving. I peek up through a small opening in my blindfold to see her removing Her panties from beneath Her skirt. Instantly I become aroused.

"Open your mouth."

I do as She commands. She stuffs Her garment in my mouth. I savor in the moment of reward. In ecstasy I lay suckling the sweet moistness from Her panties. Lost in euphoria, I lose track of Her position until I feel the burn of Her urine splattering across my open wounds. My screams are muffled in Her panties. Relieving Herself on me She says,

"This is what men like you deserve! For what you've done, you should be thankful I'm even honoring you with My presence."

With impeccable timing and control, she relieves herself with a final stream of fire across my wounds before walking out of the room, slamming the door behind Her. I am left without instructions. I lay in a pool of my own making, remembering what I've done.

I can't shower until I return home. The stench of waste from Her body teases my nostrils. I'm sour and sticky. Afraid someone will discover my shame, I drive at the speed limit, gripped with fear of being pulled over by police. I feel as if everyone driving past me knows my sins. I just want to get home.

Inside the comfort of my confines, I navigate through darkness. I want to be invisible, to shrink from existence. The light in the bathroom is on. I disrobe and stand naked before the mirror, looking at a man I despise. I smell. I haven't shaved. I'm covered in cuts and bruises. I open the medicine cabinet looking for a razor and some aspirin. I can't say I don't think of ending my life with the razor. I probably should do it with the sharp metal blade. It won't hurt much. As I contemplate my finality, a piece of paper falls from the top of the medicine cabinet. My attention is diverted.

Please read alone written on the front. The note I'd been looking for! How did it get on top of the medicine cabinet? My anticipation won't allow me to wait. I salivate at the pending discovery. I open it.

Rapid Eye Movement.

I turn the note upside down and hold it up to the light, looking for something to explain the meaning of this message. Rapid eye movement? Rapid eye movement? Her dreams? Why hadn't I thought of that before? I should have analyzed her dreams. I pound the sink with my fist. This small, but crucial piece of analysis -- I should have asked her about her dreams. I should've investigated her subconscious thoughts. Another item on the long list regrets in my relationship with her. She'd been back in my presence as a blessing, my opportunity for redemption and I blew it. Another chance to make up for the wrongs against her, gone. I toil over the things I wish I could have done. You can't change the things you've done, you can only live with them. With each day I live, I'm dying inside. My imagination, the only comfort of connection I have to be with her, but thoughts of happy times contort like a once beautiful car after an accident. No pleasant thoughts, it all ends the same. How do you remember the fun times in your favorite car without remembering the wreckage of its demise? How do you do that? Rapid eye movement?

In the shower with my sins the scorching water runs red, brown, yellow, and then clear. The lovely stench from Mistress' waste, removed. How can I be absolved without resolution? Rapid eye movement? I exit the shower, perplexed by this question. I slip on my robe still wet and walk to the kitchen to fix some warm milk. I reach for a cup in the cupboard, when something moves in the corner my eye. I turn my head and drop the cup; it shatters across the kitchen floor. In my living room, Ms. Amen.

Chapter XI: Class Resumes

I arrive on campus around 4am. It's bone chillingly cold walking into the classroom. The thermostat is not working. My breath condensing into fog as it leaves my body; thermostat reads 30°. I call maintenance, pondering the outline for this semester. The real Professor found a great awareness which should have been used to accumulate greater understanding of our fellow human beings. Instead, it was turned against him and used to convict mentally ill patients of illegal activity. I am excited to reunite with the students. The first to arrive, as expected, my new assistant, Ms. Amen.

Sent by Carl to watch over me, Ms. Amen told me the rapid eye movement message was his. He'd been watching me and I was insecure -- did he know about Mistress? I'm sure. For a blind man, he sees better than anyone I have ever known. Ms. Amen will participate in the class, as any one of my other students. Her face had become a comfort, reminding me of our connection and our purpose. When I asked her to see Carl she wrote, *We don't see Carl. He sees us. No way to contact him, but when we need him he will be there.* I receive no insight into his message, *rapid eye movement.* She didn't know what was written in the note. I would have to trust intuitive consciousness and indwelling intelligence. The rest of the students arrive.

"Class! Welcome back. I'm pleased to see you all have returned and I trust you enjoyed the winter break."

"What did you do for the break, Professor?" Mr. Macpherson makes me smile.

Images of myself in a drunken stupor, bloody, broken glass on my bathroom floor, my Mistress' exposed breasts flash through my mind. I thought about Maria. Carl. The class.

"My holiday season was dedicated to this study. The loss of our first subject interrupted our course. The loss of my assistant interrupted some organizational planning time for our curriculum. My obligation to you all is important. Confidence and trust maintains a covenant. I filled the position with this in mind. Ms. Amen is my new assistant. This isn't a test taking class, so she will not have an unfair advantage. I want the answers inside your mind for this study. Now let's review last semester's material."

I walk over to the chalkboard and write, *I know nothing.* I look them over, evaluating their responses. All of them except for one look confused.

"Ms. Emch, please explain to me what this means."

Her piercing gaze fixed on the chalkboard she says, "Professor, I don't how can I possibly know what that means."

The other students chuckle.

She remains playfully serious, her eyes hinting at a smile. I feel my heartbeat quicken and blood rush to an unwelcome place.

"Very good, Ms. Emch. You have the right answer. Do any of you know why I had you write this heading in your notes?"

He lifts his hand, I expect as much, the cynical member of the group.

"Yes, Mr. LaDay."

"Because... we don't know anything?"

He smirks without the others.

"No, Mr. LaDay. How can the meaning of the statement be the reason I asked you to write it?"

The response does little to slow his increasing smile. His taunting grin turns arrogant and challenging.

"Please enlighten the class, Mr. LaDay. Tell me how the meaning of this statement and the reason for writing it are the same?"

His grin widens at my challenge before the class, welcoming the opportunity to contend with me.

"Professor, we do not know anything and that is the meaning, your reason for having us write the statement in our notes is to further establishing a fact like an animal learning a command for human amusement. By having us write your instruction, we emphasize the point of knowing nothing before our next experience -- your instruction. Thereby its meaning and the instruction to write it are the same thing."

He seems satisfied by his response to my challenge. Confidently victorious, he awaits my defeated reply.

"Please give a show of hands for those who support Mr. LaDay's conclusion."

He smiles looks around the room. No one raises their hand. This emphasis should be sufficient to humble him, his fellow students' lack of approval. He finishes looking around the room, then back to me and says,

"See! The statement is right. They don't know anything."

" Mr. LaDay! I will not stand by and allow you to insult this class. The statement *I know nothing*, refers to our need to know. The desire people have for an answer to a question not yet posed. When you know, there's no need. When you don't know, there is a reason. I instructed you to write this as the heading for your notes because I want your minds to be open to more than just your own experiences. I don't want you to approach any part of this course with preconceived societal roles and indoctrination. Everything in this class, you are hearing for the first time. Am I clear? That's the difference between the meaning and the reason. You hear it for the first time."

His cocky grin now serious now; he nods his head.

"Yeah... Sure Professor."

I have their attention.

"Okay class let's move on to a review of our subject. As I told you before, we are gaining a better understanding of human beliefs. Our first subject suffered from a severe case of unorganized, delusional thoughts. These thoughts have a process, they come from somewhere. Ms. Rivera's beliefs have an origin, a root. These are not external concepts forced into her mind. They are internally, accepted concepts the mind, incorporated into her perceptions of the world. Where do they come from? What do they mean to the individual psyche? Let us examine."

"Ms. Thick."

"Yes Professor."

"Please tell me what our subject said, if anything, that stood out to you or struck a chord with you. Take your time. You can review your notes if you'd like."

The class laughs at the joke.

"Ah, here it is!"

They laugh a little more.

"I'm glad we are doing this review today, I wanted to talk about the things that happened with Ms. Rivera. I liked her. I could tell she is really pretty when she gets dressed up. I have a friend that looks like her. She doesn't really know how to do makeup, but she's really pretty."

"Okay, Ms. Thick. We understand. "

"Sorry, Professor. I can go on and on. The topic I found most interesting was the cycle of energy – predator versus prey. One species flourishes and another becomes extinct. I really thought about life when she said that. I know she's crazy, but that's really deep. I mean, it isn't too far from the truth. Considering she used to work as a scientist, some of her beliefs have to come from her more coherent states when some semblance of reality is present, right Professor?"

Ms. Thick only acts as if she's out of her element I never wondered about my decision in selecting her for this class.

"Ms. Thick, it is interesting you pose this particular question. Was the coherent moment in the subject's thought process a seemingly rational thought that becomes an abstract reality concept? Meaning, during lucid moments does Ms. Rivera attempt to rationalize a delusional perception? Mr. LaDay, what do you think about Ms. Thick's question?"

He is still harboring resentment from our last engagement. Not a man who easily accepts defeat. We meet at his venomous eyes,

"A person suffering from delusional thinking must find a way to rationalize their thoughts. The person suffering doesn't think they are having a delusional idea. It's not some perception the person believes to be false; they're not wrestling within their own reality to escape delusion. At the time the delusion takes place, it is as real to them as the discussion we are having in this class. The individual has a concrete belief in their perception. In the case of Ms. Rivera, she has concepts that some of us can rationally make connections to. The basis of these delusions have some merit. But her condition twists in her processing, making the basis of her merits unbelievable to her audience. This is

94

not an attempt for her to rationalize a delusional thought, this is a rational thought that she has made delusional. Right, Professor?"

I'd made the right choice in selecting him also.

"Yes, Mr. LaDay, I think you have sufficiently satisfied the question. Does anyone have any comments regarding Mr. LaDay's response?"

I study their faces; their body language. I savor the moment of stillness. Ms. Amen looks around sensing the energy shift accompanying the silence her eyes scan for the reason of inactivity. Ms. Thick didn't have anything further to say. Mr. Macpherson looming quietly, with the presence of an overseer. The ever-cocky Mr. LaDay smiles approvingly. Was he going to say more? Ms. Emch,

"Ms. Rivera's intelligence far surpasses that of our own and because of her superior intelligence, she is prone to realistic thoughts which unfortunately turn delusional to conceptually uniform thinkers. Her mind enhances what most consider reality of the moment. There's no off switch. An idea born in her mind grows outside of basic perceptions. I agree that she turns rational thoughts into delusion.

"Take her view on imaginary differences, her basic argument is strong. Given the same physical, environmental, mental, and age attributes, any human being is capable of doing the same thing with training, education, and conditioning. The winner is only dictated by the concept of time. She uses that thesis to propose that differences are imaginary. This is where the switch between reality and theory spins out of control. Her conclusion is not fact but merely an argument which needs to be properly supported, or proven false. She should have documentation of her research and investigation into her claim. This is the regular pattern someone with her type of educational background would follow. Instead, she conceptualizes obsessively, delving further into the idea and with the chemical imbalance she suffers from, her ideas become illogically twisted in her own rationale. She says, 'The media forces images of beauty on us and creates more imaginary differences.' This assertion ties into her dominant delusional about Controllers and Protectors where all of her conclusions begin and end. Thus giving the reason why she doesn't seek further research or investigation, everything is tainted by the rationalized paranoia which twist her perception. The only safe, logical conclusion she draws from any hypothesis, is in her own rational, thus constraining her ideas and concepts in a mental prison. Instead of a straight line beginning to end she goes in circle. Her superior intelligence is ultimately the reason why it will be next to impossible to bring her into any suitable level to function in society."

"A very interesting take, Ms. Emch. The mind of our subject being dominated by a premise that overrules her rational comprehension. Meaning, no thought can deviate from the dominant conviction; everything must lead back to the control belief system. Divergent thoughts conflict with and challenge our subject's beliefs and so even when faced with a rational opposing observation, she must come back to her primary belief which then causes her to warp reality in her mind creating connections that are circular in reference to the controlling belief. The prevailing thought is one of paranoia, thus she is suspicious of all outside information. Her highly educated mind can only draw comparisons, which make little sense to the linear perception. Ms. Emch?"

"Yes, Professor, that's perfect."

Away from her eyes I survey the class.

One face appears to reflect possible dissent. I deny him the platform for spectacle.

"Class! In order to satisfy sacrificing what we want, don't we all have to conjure some sort of fantasy? Our own secret fantasy revolving around our 'what ifs'? The key to invention is the fantastical possibility of something that didn't exist. Don't most people have some sort of idea or thought that can sound delusional or unrealistic to another person? The greatest creations of man were, at one time, thought to be impossible. Many inventors were shunned or called crazy. Is innovation and profound thinking born from a seemingly delusional mind? Ms. Emch thinks Ms. Rivera makes sense from nonsense and none of you objected. So I assume you all concur."

He hadn't been listening. Now I allow him to speak. The perfect fool for comic relief.

"I don't agree, Professor." In fool regalia, Mr. LaDay stands, "How can a woman with such scattered thought patterns and delusional thinking make a lot of sense? I do agree that every person holds some kind of dream-like, wishful fantasy, and this state of mind can make a seemingly normal person seem delusional. However, these unrealistic states which can lead to possible invention and profound thought are not a connection to the extreme types of delusional thinking Ms. Amen suffers from. If Ms. Amen's circular delusions make sense to someone, then that person may be having some delusions themselves."

"So what, Danny? Are you calling me delusional now because I understand the conceptual troubles she's having connecting her thoughts to reality? Am I identifying with delusional thinking because I'm crazy and that's why I'm able to understand her? Or is it because my ability to do good in this class is so superior to yours and you can't grasp this elevated level of thinking? You are the person who thought the light bulb and automobile were crazy, and I am the person who was delusional enough to create it."

My students grasp the power of the idea and why evil wishes to control it. Ms. Emch's emphasis regarding the creation of a light bulb and automobile establish her understanding of grasping a dream idea without fear of peer rejection as crazy or impossible. I interject another turn on this road of enlightenment.

"Why is history important, ladies and gentlemen?"

They look at me as if an intruder from an alien nation. The classic symptoms of the argumentative thought process.

"Come on class! Why is history important?"

A moment to contemplate the question. The shepherd down this diverted path. Mr. Macpherson.

"History is how we understand our present moment. How can we understand our present without understanding our past? The continuation of our technological society is dependent on the lessons of our prior innovations. How can we create portable communication if we haven't developed standard communication devices? What is the automobile without the invention of the combustion engine? History is far more than a story of dramatics up for interpretation by present society. History establishes the building blocks necessary for future generations to carry on the works of their predecessors. History is education; information gathered from the past for present generations to understand their place in the story. Without a history, we have to create it, right?"

A few laughs and chuckles at low levels. The class seems to digest Mr. Macpherson's interpretation of history quite well. I assume the reins of our storied travel.

"So, in considering Ms. Emch's statement about the delusional thinking of innovation, is it safe to say history's evolution is based in delusional thinking? Terms and references never created before, or, as Mr. Macpherson put it, the creation of history?"

They look confused. This discussion holds a lot of substance to digest. The tortuous path to enlightenment is the beginning go understanding. They were learning the foundations of truth. Mr. LaDay was ready,

"History is the foundation of identity. We define ourselves based on history. What's foreign to one person may be common to a group of people. Our identity is based on marks and scars from experience -- impressions. Our history is not based so much on delusion as on necessary comforts for innovation. I think our class is getting a bit off topic. We are trying to redefine a term.

"Delusion is persistent false psychotic belief. A psychotic belief is based on psychosis; a serious mental illness marked by loss of, or greatly lessened ability to test whether what one is thinking and feeling about the world is true. This means a person suffering from delusional thoughts is having a difficult time in the real world. A person suffering from delusional thinking is not having a problem explaining light bulbs and combustion engines to a group of people who have never heard of them before. A delusional person is losing their grip on reality and having a hard time applying their thoughts to realistic terms. Right, Professor?"

I give a nod of agreement. When I review the tape I still feel myself counting backwards from ten. The conflict may not be resolved, but aggravation is far from my intention. Creating discourse among a group is counter-productive, unless for stimulating independent thinking. A uniform project sees one answer, one solution, and agrees. Conflict must have opposition. Ten seconds is up. Ms. Emch reignites the tension.

"I don't agree, Danny, this discussion is not off topic. We are not redefining a term, we are understanding its complexity and its meaning. You said psychosis is a mental illness marked by a person's lessened ability to test whether what they are thinking or feeling is true. No one in this class has disagreed that Ms. Rivera is suffering from severe psychosis. We can all agree to that. The question here is our evaluation of delusional thinking. Before the study of psychology, people were not as easily diagnosed. In *The Silent Mind*, our Professor outlines this fact in the opening chapter."

She catches my eye contact briefly. I have to look away.

"How many of you have read the Professor's book?"

One person raises their hand, Ms. Amen. She looks at me again. Our eye contact is a gesture of connection, traveling this path to truth. Her powers control this phase of the journey. The silence of her peers demonstrates unanimous agreement. We were all like children going for a surprise car ride, eagerly awaiting the destination Ms. Emch would take us. She stood and walked toward the front of the class. White tennis shoes, blue jeans, a white fitted shirt to highlight her hour-glass curves. She needed no permission.

"You see class, the reason the title in our notes states we know nothing, is the very reason why we are having a discussion of this nature. Our Professor's book outlines a theory for the psychiatric world: mental illness is not objective, it's subjective. It asserts society doesn't factor the symptoms specific to individuals for each subject under evaluation of their own personal disease. We categorize and herd diagnoses thus conforming treatment, and the patient's mind is lost to assimilation under the herd diagnosis. We accept these ways because before the diagnoses of mental capacity, mentally ill people were not as easily defined. The Professor concludes his theory by saying uniform reality is based on society's environmental peer pressures. We interact in a seemingly uniform fashion however, this interaction not a standardized truth among all. Crime and protest, rampant throughout societies, are outlined in the Professor's book as the fight against conformity. He states people classified as mentally ill are simply demonstrating an opposition to conformity. They have perceptions that twist transform into, hidden desires or complex paranoia based on a dominant belief. A mentally ill person, as defined by our society, doesn't create abstract thought from objective reality. The mentally ill person takes reality and gives it a subjective understanding, which is what we all do. We see the world in our own way. From our own angle in position of space in the moment of experience. We don't all have the same desires of the moment and we thrive in the reflection of our observations – our world of appearances. This society allows us to live so many different ways: homeless, criminal, religious, celebrity, blue-collar, in positions of power, as teachers, or students, we can remain unemployed if we wish; in this society we can live however we choose. The Professor has formed an equation that finds our species capable of understanding infinite realities. If you can imagine a form of existence, no matter how bizarre to your own understanding, as long as there is time for the eternal moment to form the transitions of birth, death, and creation, that imagination has the possibility to exist at some point in the universe. The scenarios you conceive of human activity can possibly exist as someone's perceived reality. The mentally ill represent many facets of this equation. In this way, mental illness is a form of rejecting our standardized perceptions. The Professor's book outlines the understanding of this rejection as another possibility of subjective reality. He believes we can find a greater understanding of ourselves through the looking glass of standard reality rejection. Any of you who have read the Professor's book will see this class discussion is not off topic. We are not redefining a term, we are redefining understanding. You should all read the Professor's book. It's a good introduction to the world of appearances."

She returns to her seat having dropped the class off in new territory. I bide my time before speaking, still digesting her words. Evil will be severely damaged by her teachings. Mr. LaDay knew he'd been trumped, but defeat has given way to enlightenment. I hadn't written the book, but I act as if I have. I dismiss the class.

"Life is a series of events and moments that shape an individual's view of the world. It's what makes us unique. Each of us alive in our own perspective space of reality; we each experience different moments in time and occupied space. From the moment we are born into the world, we are given a specific time and space to occupy. This is an inescapable fact. No two people can occupy the same space at the same time other than mother and unborn child. When a child is born, its assignment in space and time is given. We occupy these permanent assignments in this formula: age (moment of birthed existence, into the form of reflected observation) coupled with the location of form (where your physical presence is) is your identity of perception. This simple formula is your moment of time in the universe until death. Death is the release of your essential formless energy that controls your space-form presence. The release allows for new form generations to be in the eternal-moment you once occupied.

"The formula of the individual is simple. The collective formula is much more complex. We share moments, experiences, and events. We build upon these collective experiences and pass them to one another through stories, education, and basic communication. This makes individual moments in time a collective movement. If you gather a room full of people and watch them interact, count the individual moments of action made up by the group as a whole. I scratch my head, you cross your legs, he gets up, she stretches, they talk, I wave my arms, you touch her knee, he walks across the room, she strokes her hair, they walk around. The band plays on at the stadium concert. The speed at which we move collectively is: one moment multiplied as billions of different moments moving in different spaces at the same moment in time. We can occupy the same year, same month, same day, same hour, and same second of a moment, but we cannot occupy each other's physical presence of existence. So, as we enjoy the day together we cannot enjoy the same perspective. This allows us to enjoy the day together with different understandings of that day. I'm in

London and you're in New York; I am 35 and you are 16 rotations of the Earth around the sun. To calculate the number of current possible perspectives, we begin with the age of each living person, we factor their various positions on Earth since birth, and apply it to each individual's experiences. This will give us the number of mental realities possible on Earth and then the number will change the very second we are done, just due to life and death constantly altering the number of people on earth. We don't use the human population of Earth to receive the answer of possible realities because every individual's perspective reality experience is constantly changing by the moment. We are not frozen in one experience.

"Individual reality is constantly one circumstance, one second, one moment away from a new experience, every second of each individual's life must be added, and then that number added to the collective age of every human in existence at that moment. The scope of human existence is based on the confines of what the individual's culture and surroundings allow in that time. A predominately industrial society allows for only so many possibilities for one individual, just as a predominately rural area allows for only so many possibilities for another individual. We have to divide that number by the factored environments of the time, to give us the number of duplicate realities, reducing the number of possible realities. Many of us share experiences with others at the same time without truly being aware of it. Hundreds, thousands, or even millions of people do the same thing at the exact same moment. While I'm eating, millions of others are eating and some are possibly eating the exact same thing. Millions of us watch television programs at the same time. I may stop watching television to use the bathroom, and 100 other people may do the same thing. We are living in different times of space factored into this equation individually, but the division is to eliminate duplicating experiences. My math is a bit rough, but there are approximately 56 trillion different possible human observed perceptions of experiences in a one-year period on Earth. Given this enormous number, we cannot fathom all of the possible perceptions happening in the world. This is why we cannot grasp mental illness. Mental illness is part of this

102

equation. In fact, I believe it makes up the top echelon of possibilities. This equation reaches the human mind so far beyond the scope of understanding that we write off our inability to comprehend with the label of "mentally ill". We generalize these far-reaching realities as illness because we can't accept their delusions and unorganized thoughts. We don't accept the "mentally-ill" view of the world, and when the collective understanding doesn't share the popular experience in human society, majority tends to rule. We collectively rule out things we don't understand and this is a constraint on grasping reality. We crush and suppress our desires to fit in with the collective. We form our ideas under our societies' passed-down beliefs and only advance the collective idea, or rebel against an idea, based on the foundation of principles we are collectively taught to believe.

"Our collective beliefs are so far from the essence of our natural origins that we may need to re-evaluate what beliefs we are placing before ourselves. Some individuals simply cannot conform to the collective beliefs."

The original Professor had cracked the surface of Truth with only his mind to guide him. He understood why Maria's existence wasn't a label to be generalized and cast away. She was another reality examined against all we'd been taught. Yes, there are people who suffer from uncontrollable delusions and disorganized thinking. The Professor's book asks why mentally ill people are dealing with reality so abstract from our own. He offers questions to stimulate thought outside of what we believe and enter the possibility of understanding the beliefs of others. Like Maria, others hold the Truth outside our teachings and understanding. The pressure to conform to society's teachings and not stray from it limits our scope of true reality, like those who believed the world was flat. We hold ourselves captive by our collective teachings and because of their control, we never veer too far from inherited lessons. Even our revolutions don't change the progression. We simply continue to build on top of what we've already been taught. As the Professor stated in his book, we could learn a lot about free thought from someone we label mentally ill.

I doze off thinking about how things would be if we weren't on this path. I dream of flying through the sky with Maria by my side in the form of eagles.

Chapter XII: Second Subject

The convalescent home's odor is one of sterilizing chemicals mingling with the treatments that accompany advanced human aging. Elderly men and women roam the halls with no obvious destination. My students follow me in silence. It is a very different entrance experience than our visits to Maria at the hospital. I don't know how to interpret their collective silence other than equating the lack of frivolous conversations and nervous behaviors to means growth -- another step closer to a new subject.

The collective thought of our modern belief is an evolution from something unimaginable to our predecessors. The original Professor's work made this a key point for the basis of his theory. *Our reality of fast-moving technological innovation and highly complex social interactions are promoting a functional insanity. Not everyone is capable of conforming to our established customs and rules. A chemical imbalance in the mind could impede one's efforts to conform and assimilate into these societal roles and function. This marks their descent into madness. Those of us who accept the world around us without question do not understand those who question the world. A singular view of the world without question is ignorance, but a world en masse without question is insane.* In studying Mr. Clark, a man who's lived over a century, we will learn the next piece to this puzzle in picturing humanity. We meet with some of the managing staff at the convalescent home and are briefed on our subject. The 115-year-old man's physical health in good condition considering he's the second oldest living person in the world; his mental health is a different story. He suffers from dementia; a result of Alzheimer's. His cognitive reasoning had diminished dramatically in a short period of time. He rambles about the world being controlled by an alien race of people who are cousins to human beings. He views our technological innovation as tools to control humanity, making us weak and dependent on the alien race for survival.

What had enlightened him? I am eager to see him face to face.

Again Ms. Amen accompanies me while the other students watch and listen from monitors in another room.

As we approach the door a rush of excitement flushes over me. I knock and wait for a response.

An elderly voice, "Who is it?"

"Me, Gene."

He pauses.

"Oh... What took so long? Come in."

I open the door to see him in a wheelchair facing a window overlooking a courtyard. He doesn't turn to face us when we enter.

"Close the door," he says.

With my eyes locked on him I close the door. I don't know what to expect. I feel the honor of being in his presence; my subjective feelings of celebrity toward another human being. Some people may not care they're in the presence of the second oldest living human being, but I do. His wisdom, his experiences, his ideas, his day-to-day activities are an astonishing study of human activity. He is not just another old man occupying a space eager for youthful change. Ms. Amen's eyes projected that she felt it too; we are in the presence of greatness. Standing behind him, I look through the window to see from his perspective. He does not turn around. The images outside the window contain no special significance; in fact, there's very little activity at all, a groundskeeper trims the hedges, a staff member walks across the patio. I wonder what he's thinking. He utters,

"All news comes from the same source. They call it the Associated Press. In my early days, news came from whoever got it first. Reporters were always looking for a story, even if they had to make it up." He chuckles, "I remember hearing a broadcast about aliens landing and being scared out of my wits. I wasn't alone. My whole family, my whole town, hell, the whole dang country was terrified. Those were the good ole days. We thought aliens had taken over the world. Our imaginations ran wild. I expected to see octopus looking things with tentacles standing over me when I woke up. Some of my neighbors were fleeing from their homes in search of refuge. Some stayed to fight for their homes and their way of life. My father was

106

one of those people who stayed to fight. I remember watching people run and holler -- the doggone craziest thing you ever saw! Folks scattered about everywhere. Some were too terrified to even come out of their homes. My father and another group of men rode around patrolling the neighborhood looking for aliens and people who needed help. He gave me a six shot pistol and told me I was the man of the house until he came back. He put me in charge of protecting my mama and my little brother. That night was brought to us by a toothpaste company," he laughs again, "Can you believe that? A gawd dang toothpaste company scared half the country out of their wits. My mama cried her eyes out that night thinking my father was never coming back home. I don't even think those people apologized for what they'd done... Come to think of it they did, but it didn't mean nothing. My Pa never bought that toothpaste again and if we ever used it or mentioned that name he'd tan our hides."

Silence. He stared out the window -- a silent moment with the second oldest living person. His every word, a moment for reflection. He continued,

"I think that was their first test to see if they could control and move us at will. My Ma didn't want us to listen to the radio alone at night in our room anymore. She thought they were going to poison our minds against her." He pauses. "Now in my recollection she might have been onto something. The way these kids are today with their disrespect, it's a shame. Our town saw maybe one bank robbery in forty years and that was from some out-of-towners. Occasionally a kid might steal a piece of candy or a toy from the general store. That was it! My Ma said those boys only robbed that bank because they listened to the radio too much. Gangsters and bank robbers glamorized. My Pa despised those types. He said, 'A man has a duty to his town and his family and taking what's not yours is for cowards and scavengers.' I always believed that. As I watched this world grow greedy and untrusting, I always wondered why more men turned to evil against each other. When I think back to that alien broadcast, I still believe aliens really did land. Maybe those aliens really took over, 'cause from where I'm sitting, I don't see many of the same kind of people I used to see. People nowadays seem more alien than human. I heard they grow babies in laboratories now. My Ma would have a heart attack if she knew they could do that. We thought babies came by the stork when we were kids. We saw pregnant ladies, but we just didn't know how the babies came out. It sure was fun to think like that." He laughs again. "They took that from us. Wars are on TV now. They broadcast everything. They broadcast the same thing. I turn to another news channel and it's the same. Local news has a bit of different stories. Sure it still has some of that nationwide, worldwide update stuff, but sometimes you can still hear about a kitten rescued from tree by a fire fighter. I don't watch it much anymore. Found myself watching too much of it in my 80's. I turned 90, and pretty much gave it up. Remember Vern, you're never too old to try something new."

The name Vern from his background report. Vern was his younger brother who had been killed in battle during World War II. Mr. Clark was beginning to dissociate due to his Alzheimer's. I don't interrupt him.

"Remember when they started putting freeways all over the place? I think that was a bad idea too. Too many strangers. Big cities are overrated. When I moved from home to go to college I hated it. Remember? I wrote Ma and called home every chance I could. Those dang city people were always doing their best to make me homesick. I almost quit and move back home. That small town, know your neighbors life always made me comfortable. Cities ruin hospitality and manners. Too many strangers. Think about it, Vern. Those big fancy cities are accidents waiting to happen. Cut off the power supply and watch the people clog the streets in a crazed panic. Those big cities depend on people staying inside their homes and jobs. You can't have eight million people outside at one time in one city. You remember trying to drive a car through that, Vern? Remember when that storm came? All those people cut off from electricity. Couldn't go to the supermarket. Couldn't plug into their gadgets. People came outside their comforts and realized they didn't even know their neighbors. It's just like Ma used to tell us, 'If it didn't come in a bag most people wouldn't even trust it.' That's the problem nowadays, Vern.

"They have us strung out. We don't do anything for ourselves anymore. Everything is done for us. That's what's wrong with those cities. When I was at college, them city people always thought I was crazy. Country is what they called me. I remember Ma knitted a whole bunch of sweaters and trousers for the winter. All those fancy city kids with their name brand clothes thought I was common for wearing garments that weren't in their fashion. They joked and laughed at me because I wasn't in their style. It made me feel bad. I kind of got mad at Ma. I wrote her a letter telling her I wanted to keep a few extra dollars that month instead of sending it to the bank so I could get an outfit for a party some kids at school were throwing. At the time, I wasn't thinking about the things I think about now, or I probably wouldn't have written the letter. You know Vern? We respected our parents' feelings back then. Right or wrong, we bit our tongues and never did anything to disrespect them or hurt them. I didn't want to come out and tell Ma I wasn't happy with the clothes I had and that those fancy city kids were teasing me because of my homemade clothing. So I told her indirectly with the letter. At the time I felt good about what I had done. I felt independent. Young people get a sense of reward when they break away from previous generations to explore their own ideas. That's how I felt. I felt independent from the country bumpkin life we'd been taught to live and love. I wanted to be like those fancy city kids. They had status and importance. I started saving money to buy my new fancy duds, and it didn't take long for me to get 'em. I went and got a get-up I'd seen one of those movie stars in. Oh, Vern, you should've seen me. I looked like a fool. I felt like one too. I look like a pig in a wig. It just wasn't me and the city kids were laughing even harder than they were before. I'd spent a good amount of my money on those fancy name brand duds. I felt stupid. Then finally Ma's letter came. I'll never forget it. She said, 'Suga Plum,' I always liked it when she called me that, 'you don't need fancy clothes to prove who you are. Those kids are twisted up chasing pictures instead of making pictures. They're buying things because they're told to. The clothes you're wearing were made with your Mama's hands to clothe your body and keep you warm. It's not the clothes; it's who's wearing the 'em.'

"That letter made me realize what fashion really was. Fashion was another tool. I'd spent my hard earned money on fashion to make some designer rich. I could've sent that money to Mama. I wrote a report on that for school and got an A. Fashion, I never wore advertised clothes or shopped at fancy, stylish stores ever again. I shopped at places where regular people made clothes. No fancy designers. Just regular people, tailors.

"No more of those fancy threads and I walked to class with my head held high. No shoes or socks, my bare feet on the grass that started a trend. City folk are really impressionable like that. This one real uptight fella took his shoes and socks off and walked on the concrete. Maybe he had something to prove by watching me and my walk on the grass. Nevertheless it was pretty funny. I just liked feeling the wet grass in the summer. We don't water grass in the summer back home. I saw that grass, took my shoes off and walked to a nice place to sit and read my schoolbooks.

"I always loved how Ma would bring sense to the crazy. I still have a few of those old sweaters she knitted for the winter. They keep you dang warm too. She only used the wool woven by Ms. Jackson. She wouldn't use any other. Ma didn't trust those big corporations, they only want a dollar. They'll sell you stuff that don't even work just to get your hard earned money. I bet those fancy threads them city kids had didn't last over 90 years like Ma's hand-knit sweaters. I never used a moth ball in my life. Seems like the moths didn't want to touch Ma's sweaters."

The nurse enters the room quietly so as not to interrupt him. She whispers in my ear we need to wrap up the session, our hour was almost over and Mr. Clark's exercise and medication time fast approaching. In recognition I nod and she exits the room as quietly as she came.

"I don't care for those corporations. I know they don't care for me. Ms. Jackson cared for Ma. She came over and helped around the farm when Ma got sick. And when Pa couldn't get any work. Ms. Jackson gave him some work to do around her place. You can't get help like that from a fancy corporation. Now that was service. They don't make too many people like that anymore, Vern..." He sighs, "The good old days, huh... I guess it's time for you to be going. That nurse ain't as quiet as she thinks she is. Plus, when you get to be my age, you know what time it is without a clock. When you coming back?"

I marvel at his observance of the nurse's entrance and exit.

"Did you hear me, Vern? You're a young man. Don't tell me your ears are going."

"No Gene, I heard you. I'll be back in a couple of days. You rest up."

"You know I'm a restless spirit, I'll be here when you get back. Drive safe."

"All right, I will."

Ms. Amen and I exit without Mr. Clark ever turning around. He never took his face from the window.

My students await class, eager to discuss our first session with Mr. Clark. They are deep in discussion as I enter Mr. LaDay and Ms. Emch are going back and forth, with comments from Ms. Thick egging them both on. Mr. LaDay professes,

"The old man's not crazy or demented, he's just old. He knew when the nurse came in and out of the room without even turning around or stopping his ramblings. He continued like he hadn't noticed anything. Then, he digressed into another demented state, but acknowledged his age by saying he's had his mother's woven sweaters for 90 years. How can a man be talking to a brother who died 80 years ago while acknowledging things wrong in the present day? If you ask me, the old man's playing all of us. He's not nearly as sick as Ms. Rivera."

Ms. Emch retorts, "Danny, nobody's asking you anything. How can you deduce anything after one session? Your dime store psychology is not necessary for this class. If you listen with an open mind, you'll dive into his psyche rather than label and judge him. We are not trying to identify him. We are trying to understand him."

Ms. Thick chimes in, "Yeah, Danny! We are not trying to label him."

"You two girls are getting on my nerves with this no labels stuff. I'm not labeling him. I'm just calling it how I see it."

I interrupt, "How do you see it?"

He pauses for a moment regroups and answers head on, as I knew he would.

"Mr. Clark isn't nearly as sick as Ms. Rivera. She suffers from much deeper psychological issues and this class is not benefiting from the lighter study of Mr. Clark. It's like going backwards instead of going to the next level. Since we can't complete our study of Ms. Rivera, we should choose a subject who equals our level of study. This old man is just going to give us a bunch of stories about the good ol' days mixed in with a bit of disassociation. I mean, come on! What are we going to truly accomplished by studying this old guy? It's not as if he's going to benefit or recover from his Alzheimer's. What's the point?"

I look around the class to examine their faces. The other students absorb his remarks. His point well made. Mr. Macpherson,

"Danny, do you get how much of an honor it is to be able to speak with the second oldest living person? Only one other person alive has lived longer than him. I'll admit he's not as sick as Ms. Rivera, but he is a fitting subject for this class. Already he's allowed us a look into how human experience has changed over his lifetime. He showed us the evolution of mass psyche in one story. That, in itself, is something worth discovering. You should be honored Danny. You should take this as a privilege and honor rather than a task."

Absorb the other side of the coin, provided by Mr. Macpherson.

We devise our strategy for the next session with Mr. Clark. The class digs deeper into the transformation of human existence. I'm relieved.

As the class lets out, I stopped as I notice a familiar face: the curly haired woman whom I'd seen before with Ms. Emch and on the first day of class. She's watching me from the hall.

Chapter XIII: Bad News

"The struggle for life and the struggle for power live in the same place. I don't know what all the fuss is about. If you ask me, society's become too complicated. Yeah, it's always been some person who wants to be in charge. From two individuals to two billion, someone's always trying to figure out how to be the important one. That's nature I guess.

"When I was a boy we had this pig I named Matilda. Now Matilda wasn't your average pig. She had this mean streak in her and she was real big. I mean *big* -- and nasty. She was so mean we used to have to take her out of the pen so the other pigs could eat. She wouldn't even let her own young eat. Now that I think about it, I don't know if she was mean or just greedy... maybe both. Whatever it was, she sure did taste good. We ate links, ribs, sausages, bacon, and fried skins. Ah, Matilda.

"See, it don't really matter how greedy, mean, or driven you are. There's always somebody waiting to eat you. That's nature. It don't matter how well you size it up, that's the bottom line. Those high-tech leaders with their formulas and social models just complicate everything. These wars today are frivolous zoning issues, people meddling in other people's affairs. If you don't like how another country is being to their citizens then offer them refuge but don't meddle in their political divisions. We use to fight to protect our way of life. Now we fight for control, and we inject our way of life. I'd respect it more if they openly admitted trying to conquer the world or something. How would we like it if another country came here and told us they support one of our political parties versus all others then started bombing our homes? They fool us into believing that our kids are dying for something. Send thousands of them off to die over a difference in opinion. Jerk number one goes back to the citizens with a trumped up lie about what jerk number two and their citizens are doing. It's so much dang noise in everybody's ears that the truth can't be heard. And the citizens are rallied into a trap. You know, I've been around a long time, but I've never seen one of those jerks go off and fight a war side by side with their troops. I think they wouldn't be so trigger-happy then."

Mr. Clarks stares out of his window still as he talks; he's yet to look in our direction. The subject of war seems to trouble him a great deal. In the memories of a person who's lived a long life one question unlocks a wealth of information. Ms. Emch put it best when she referred to our older citizens as time capsules; treasure chests of moments gone by.

He continues on the topic of war.

"When me and you were lil' kids we used to play with army men all day and all night. We built war scenes in the dirt, in the barns, in the trees, in our rooms. Hell, we made a war scene in the kitchen. Ma chased us out of the kitchen quick. We never did that again, huh Vern? We created our own little world with those army men. We'd do heroic things with them army men like save villages, kids, and women, stuff like that. We weren't thinking about oil rights and big business. We just thought about being heroes for our country. We didn't dare disturb Pa in the living room. I thought that's what soldiers were supposed to be: our protectors, our defenders, our saviors. We didn't even know the toy army men we played with were part of a government program to introduce kids to war. We just wanted to play with the toys, and we played right along. I'll never forget the day you told me you wanted to be a Marine, Vern. You couldn't have been no more than nine-years-old. The sparkle in your eyes when you said it could have brightened the entire sky. I said, 'me too' just cause you said it, but I wasn't as serious as you. A few years later, I wanted to be a fireman but you still wanted to be a Marine. You turned 18 and went right into the forces to become Marine. I always thought, *Man! Here's a guy who knew what he wanted to become became what he wanted to be and he was proud to be what he'd become.* I held a bit of envy about that." He said with a laugh. "Here I am a successful student in college on my way to law school and I'm envious of my kid brother who's an enlisted man in the Marines. Sound crazy? ...Maybe. Depending on whose standards are applied. It's crazy to me because my Ma used to say 'Envy is when you ain't doing something you ain't

114

supposed to be doing but wishing you could.' She always had a way with words. I find myself thinking about that statement. When people are jealous of each other they want to do things the other person is doing. If a person were able to do what another person does, or have what the other person is having, would they want it as much? So here I am not doing something I'm not supposed to be doing in the first place. I wasn't a soldier in physical combat but as a lawyer I became a soldier for rights and proofs of society. Ma was real wise. She only went to school till the third grade. With a law degree and having outlived just about everybody on Earth I'm still just coming to understand some of the things that woman taught me. 'Books are not everything,' she used to say, 'you could learn a lot by just watching the world around you.' That saying served me well as a judge. It don't ease my guilt at night. You know, man's not meant to carry all of those deeds and such from other people's lives. War... Laws..."

He falls quiet, staring out of his window. I know the review of his life can't be easy. The time he's spent far outstretches the time he has left. The medication begins wearing off. His thoughts get away from him. Ms. Amen taps my arm and signals to her watch. Our time for this session is over. Before I can speak,

"It's best you two be getting along. The nurse is probably pacing a hole in the floor outside waiting on you. I can feel my crazy talk coming. I'll see you soon."

Ms. Amen and I excuse ourselves to find the anxious nurse pacing the floor just as he'd said.

When bad news comes, you can feel it sometimes. My eyes wide open to the late-night talk show muted on my television. My mental review of Mr. Clark's session fills my silence in the room. As I compile notes for my class sleep begins to fill my thoughts with cloudy reasoning. I know if I doze off I'll lose track of everything around me. I see Ms. Amen. I don't check the TV. I don't check my watch, she startled me. Her hand extends toward me with a note. I grab it and open it.

115

Your daughter is alive. We have her in a safe place.

As for Maria, we were unable to find her. Hospital records, I'm sorry to say, list her disappearance as suicide. A source at the hospital confirms a woman matching Maria's description was found dead in her room. Disposal of her remains has been listed as cremated.

I'm sorry, my friend. I hope you can find comfort in knowing your daughter is alive. I will contact you in person soon. Continue on. It's what she would want. Peace and blessings upon you. —Carl

Silence. My hand trembles gripping this life-altering piece of paper. When I look back on this day I don't know if I dozed off before my nightmare. It just feels like I can't wake up. Ms. Amen didn't stay to comfort me after I read the message. She disappeared. Maria had taken her own life? There has to be some mistake. The woman I know wouldn't have done something like that. She wouldn't have left this world, our daughter, me like this. She knew our daughter needed her. I know her pain had to be great, but I know she wouldn't take her own life. Something else had to be at work here.

I find myself on autopilot. Everything seems like a movie. I stand in front of the hospital. I don't remember driving. I only remember being here. I remember talking to the nurses, but I don't remember exactly what they said. I remember the word 'sorry' and I remember the word 'dead'. I remember my car. I remember fog inside my head. Pain. Sharp-stinging pain. Have you ever felt a pain so deep inside yourself that it takes over who you are? A pain that kills the person you were and leaves you with a person you don't want to be? An aching, nagging cramp that won't go away? Not a pain you heal; a pain you live with. It never goes away. Lost love. Love lost.

I stare at my class. Sleep hasn't found me. I keep no pictures of Maria for fear they would find them. The only images I have of her are the ones in my mind. Thoughts of days gone by burned into my memory. The countless hours we spent together. I hold nothing of her but these memories. Memories that haunt me. Even as I stand before my class, I cannot stop thinking about her. I can't reason anything. My mind is being fried by the haunting slideshow of the life I've lived. I can't be who I was born being; I am what they want me to be, what they tell me I was born to be.

"Professor, do you think our wars are rooted in greed, or do you think they're born from a sense of protection on some level?"

The lovely Traci Thick maintains a childlike innocence which conceals her cunning. She easily lowers the defenses of men, disarming them to do her bidding.

"Ms. Thick, your question is too complex for a simple answer. It requires discussion. I will begin with my thoughts but anyone who wants to share will have the same opportunity.

"Wars are the result of two opposing forces. A military operation with little resistance is an invasion. Wars are primarily fought over protection of something. There have always been spoils of war. On some level, greed plays a part for the victor. Some type of incentive is present. Now, if your question pertains to this country, your question should be: *Does this country operate from a position of protection or greed?* What do you each think?"

I scan the room as though I don't know who I'll be selecting. I pause for effect.

"Mr. Macpherson, tell us your views on this country's underlying premise of war. Protection or greed?"

Mr. Macpherson looks into my eyes nodding his head, he accepts the invitation to state his position to the class.

"Well Professor, I've never known any soldiers, but I've watched enough television to see how war affects families. Mr. Clark spoke with great pain as he relived his brother's enlistment in the Marines. To answer your question though, I'm not sure if the citizens of our country ever know the true meaning or reason of war. Some aristocratic politician that we've elected to be in charge of us decides what's best. It's really winner take all, because most of the time a large number of citizens don't want war. We have been never invaded, so we can't base our wars solely on protection. Maybe we can say were trying to protect our way of life by eliminating a potential threat, but where does that end? If the only label we need is potential threat then a greedy person can use that label to dress up their cause to look righteous to the citizens they represent. Anybody or anything can be a potential threat if properly presented. I'm not sure what to believe anymore. All I know is that we don't know anything for certain."

The class chuckles at the irony of his statement; all but one looks pleased with the statement.

"Good answer, good answer. We know nothing for certain. Ms. Thick, please enlighten us with your take."

On the verge of tears, she redirects her energy into a gushing stream of words.

"My brother died in a military operation. He enlisted in the Army. They were there to eliminate some dictator who, as Wesley stated, could have been perceived as a potential threat. My brother's unit bombed a home that his superiors believed belonged to rebel fighters. It turned out to be a school. My brother ran into the building to save the children. He got most of them out. He went back to get the rest of them and the roof collapsed. His body was found protecting the bodies of the few remaining children in the building; they didn't make it either. This is what war brought to me. This supposed threat, the dictator, had been educated by our schools, trained by our government, and placed in power by the same politician who labeled him a potential threat. The politician rallied our citizens with a fear campaign, propaganda against future terror saying the dictator held weapons which were a threat to our country and others who believed in our way of life. You all know the story. No weapon of that capability was ever found. A corporation, once run by the politician, took control of 80% of the opposed country's natural resources. That company still controls those resources today.

"The last time I spoke with my brother, he told me we were doing good work and he believed in the mission. He dreamed of being one of the heroes who helped to liberate the people. He knew he might not come home, but he never showed any fear. When I cried to him about how I didn't want to lose him, he told me not to worry, he said he'd rather die a hero than an old man who never fought or stood for anything. That was it. My mom never showed me the letter he wrote talking about how the people there hated our military presence. How some would throw rocks and hurl insults at our soldiers. He couldn't understand; he thought that people wanted to be liberated, but they claimed to be invaded. His commanders told him that the people were unable to comprehend what was happening and that the mission would someday be appreciated. My brother died wondering if that was true.

"That was my brother's last letter to my mother. I wasn't supposed to see it; I found it postmarked a few days before his death. My mother hid it in her dresser drawer. She didn't want any of us to know about it. I never questioned her about it and to this day I never told her I know it exists. I figure if she wants me to know about it, she will tell me when the time is right. Still, I don't understand how someone can live with themselves collecting money from a company built on the blood of our young soldiers. I don't understand it. Why? It feels like I'm the only one who noticed the trick the politicians played on the citizens. Weapons of mass destruction? What weapon? The people of that country are now in disarray. For what? There are other countries with dangerous dictators. Why are we at war with a select few dictators of evil and not all? Why is my brother dead?"

The Dean enters the room and whispers the dreadful news I already know. The echo. Maria. My pain renewed. I tell him I'll speak with him after class. I look at Ms. Amen, then to the rest of the class.

"Something has just come to my attention which requires my immediate action. We will resume this discussion tomorrow. Class is dismissed for the day."

"Will we be going to see Mr. Clark tomorrow?"

Mr. LaDay's interest gives me a smile.

"No, Mr. LaDay, we will resume our sessions with Mr. Clark next week."

As I put my things away, I notice Ms. Thick doing the same. She turns to me staring softly for a moment I mouth the words, *thank you*. She nods and finishes putting her things away.

The Dean wasn't in his office. He stepped out for a minute. His secretary tells me I can wait in his office. I decline. She insists the Dean requested for me to wait there. In a daze, I enter his office to wait. I don't recognize the vision before me as reality. Carl. Discretion is good. I haven't smiled in so long. I rush to hug my friend. He embraces me.

"Carl, what brings you?"

He sighs heavily his smile fades, taking mine.

"There's trouble. Someone is inquiring into your history, investigating you, my friend. We don't know who it is. They're using fictitious credentials. It might be harmless, but someone is definitely making a serious effort to find out who the Professor is. Our people are on it, but it's possible you may not be able to finish your work here. We'll have to pull you out if it's them. You're far too important to be captured. You're a weapon for us in this war of truth. We need you to build and create more like you. You can reach those who don't know. We must stop the construction of this beast. We are feeding it with our lives."

The dean enters.

"I'm glad you made it, Professor."

"Yes, yes, I have much to say and I know we have very little time. I – I need to know about my daughter. Will I be able to see her soon?"

Carl and the dean look at one another. Then to me. The dean's eyes fall to the floor. Carl says,

"Old friend, we aren't going to be able to bring you two together. It's just too dangerous. She is precious to the cause."

I recoil.

"Precious to our cause? My daughter! What are you saying to me? She's all I have left of Maria."

I pull away from him, putting my back against the wall.

"Your daughter holds the key to the bloodline. The secret bloodline she –"

"What the hell are you talking about? The bloodline of what?"

He sighs.

"There's a lot you don't know. The first mother is the original keeper of the Truth. Her descendants are humanity. As you know, the leaders of family faces Mongoloid, Negroid, and Caucasoid maintain the covenant to protect the Truth. They worship the essence of the first human mother. "

"What does my daughter have to do with all of this?"

"She unites the bloodline."

"What? I'm not part African and Maria is Spanish."

"I know. The Dean will explain this part to you better."

"Professor! This is an amazing event. The power faction of the family has been searching for the missing portion of bloodline for centuries. And we've found it! They found it first, but their mistrustful greed of each other couldn't keep it a secret and we discovered it."

"What you're talking about? You haven't said anything more than Carl has."

"Okay, okay, listen... The bloodline is broken into three parts. Each of the three parts holds a certain power in the keys to human life. Two of the three parts co-exist and share power in directing the majority of human civilization. The third part has been missing for a long time, thousands of years. Previously, the part in hiding ruled for many millennia while the other two played subordinate roles in moving and protecting our existence. The two subordinate parts banded together and attacked, but the dominant knew they were coming and went into hiding. The two remaining parts have been in control ever since, but they live in fear of the prophecy, which comes with the new mother. When the original mother is reborn it will be time to build the mother ship. This marks the end of their rule and control. They want her to not exist."

"Okay, I am – I'm having a really difficult time understanding this. I think we're having a division of understanding. First, why would someone in control be afraid of someone in hiding who basically controls nothing? Second, this has nothing to do with the Truth. I'm not teaching my students anything different than we discussed and agreed to. Finally neither of you have told me what this has to do with me, Maria, and our daughter."

They both look at each other again.

"The reason the ones in control are afraid," the dean says, "is because the mixture of all three unlocks the power. The Supreme

Mother will walk the Earth again and cleanse this way of life. The doomsday theory in Revelations. Supreme will cleanse the Earth and we will start over again with a new way of life. The Controllers don't want this cause they hold all of the secrets just one step away from becoming extraterrestrial – like the originals. So, to eradicate the missing bloodline and hold off the birth of the Queen Mother--"

Carl cuts in.

"This all has to do with the fundamentals of what you're teaching. You see, the underground is part of the family."

"What?"

"Yes, the great separation. It took place long ago. We fight to combine the bloodlines so that the Supreme can walk the Earth again. They fight to stop it."

"What? You said that means a cleansing. People dying? That's not the Truth I teach. Aren't we the good ones?"

"We are." Carl answers, "There are just too many infected people; this has to be the way friend. We have to rid the Earth of those who cannot be saved. There are many who cannot go with us. It's no fault of their own. We do not place blame. Those infected by the Beast must be cleansed or destroyed. We cannot make the change with anyone who's been infected. They will only carry the Beast in their hearts and work to rebuild it."

"Yes, yes, I know what the Beast is."

"Then, old friend, understand what it's going to take to destroy it completely. Your students are the ones you are rescuing for redemption."

I teach the truth to disinfect people and spare them from the great cleansing? My students are those worthy of the great lesson? We support the cleansing by not trying to stop it. I thought we could save humanity. I feel tricked.

"You told me our disciples would go around spreading the truth to those who are worthy and eventually overthrow the Royals of the human Family. You never said anything about our protecting a bloodline. You never said anything about Maria and my daughter being part of a bloodline. You never said anything about taking my daughter and never allowing me to see her again. Even now, you have not told me the reason for her remaining hidden from me as her father. How am I supposed to trust anything you say? You're just as bad as the people you claim to want to destroy. Explain to me how this Truth and our mission isn't the same as the Controllers'!"

"I admit my wrong friend. I should've told you about your wife and daughter being part of the royals before your first session, but I couldn't. We didn't know if you could handle the information and still do your job. We didn't want you to be nervous or anxious because we are being watched very closely. The depth of your mission does not concern the bloodline. That would interfere with your work. The students need not know about this to be saved. All they need to do is identify the infection of the Beast. Are we clear?"

I turn to open the door.

"Dean, I will be late tomorrow. Please tell the class."

I exit before he can reply.

Life changes in an instant. My reality changed in just a few breaths. Maria dead, my daughter missing, and this Truth I'm forced to carry is the reason. I'm captive, trapped in this never-ending moment. Only a few remain uninfected. Less than one-tenth of the human population is eligible to be spared cleansing. I'm supposed to be the antidote for only a few to this poison that ravages the world? Open ears and enlightened minds comprehend my message, and beware this message can be turned against the chosen. Here, in the belly of the Beast, our work must be done.

In the indigenous places of Earth the people are uninfected. Without education in the finest institutions, they see the Truth of humanity. They see the City Beast and its nature of feeding on the life times of human beings. You don't need fancy college professors or scientists to see our alien society is far removed from natural earth. Our comforts and conveniences have made us weak and dependent on a master who uses our dependency to control us. Rural and indigenous people will not be affected by the city's demise. Our arrogance about primitive lifestyles highlights our foolishness. All of our enhancements will lead to our demise because of the power invention holds over nature and illusions. Many of us already know this subconsciously. It's why stress, depression, and insanity run rampant throughout the city. We take drugs to cope with everyday life. We are addicted to distractions. Most people can't slow down and be quiet because they don't want to deal with the reflections of their own thoughts. The more meaningless distractions we give meaning to, the less time we have to face the conflicts between the world outside us and the world inside us – suicide. Maria. Suicide?

I sink into the pain I've been seeking. My wrists and arms are tied to a suspension bar. My hour with Mistress is almost over. Metal clothespins pinching my nipples. My penis and scrotum are bound by a thin nylon rope that denies any hope of a pleasurable erection. Any arousal causes the rope to tighten on my testicles and the shaft of my penis. The weights hanging from the rope further emphasize my purgatory of arousal. She slaps my face with Her bare hand, then quickly whips my back, stomach, chest, thighs, calves, and the bottoms of my feet with Her crop. She hits my chest and the riding crop catches the clothespins ripping them from my nipples. The pain is exquisite. She slaps my chest a few times with Her open hand before replacing the clothespins on my raw nipples. My engorged penis fights hard against its bondage. The ropes are too secure and my arousal only proves to be a reminder of my predicament. She walks up to me and spits in my face.

"Maria... I'm – I'm sorry." I whisper under my breath.

She spits in my face again. I can taste it.

"You don't deserve to be sorry you bastard! Look what you've done!"

Memories of happy times and images of Maria in a straitjacket mingle in my mind. Suicide. My God! What have I done? The woman I love. I smell smoke. I think of my daughter. I think I saw her that night at Dr. Mace's home. The smoke in my nostrils chokes me, ripping from my thoughts, causing me to cough. Struggling to find breath, I smell the singed hair and burning flesh before my brain registers the searing

124

sensation of Her lit cigarette. She pulls it away, spitting on the wound left by Her extinguishing cigarette.

"That's what you deserve."

The cable holding the suspension bar is released. I crash to the floor. A clothespin flies off my body. She pushes Her heeled boot into my welted back and presses me into the floor. Another clothespin comes off. My wrists remain in their shackles. She attaches a flat leather collar around my neck.

"Crawl!" She instructs, pulling the chain attached to the collar.

I meet Her demand as best I can in handcuffs. I dare not stumble for fear of disappointing Her. She leads me down a hallway filled with screams. Hell! I am in Hell, a personal Hell of my own making. I bring to this place my sins; sins that have controlled me long since being committed. We come to the bathroom.

"Crawl in the bathtub and lay on your back."

I do as I am told with great difficulty. It hurts. I lay on my back. She takes off Her panties. The pain of my arousal burns against the rope on my genitals. I want Her to place that sweet spot on top of me. Her approval. So long without a tender touch.

"Open your mouth," she says.

I do as I am told. Her vagina's golden nectar sprinkles my face and trickles into my mouth. I dare not move my lips together as I drink the sweet waste of Her body. This is the only thing I am fit to deserve from a woman after what I've done to the women in my life.

"Lick your lips. That's a good boy. I'll bring you your clothes. Don't you dare move while I'm gone."

No matter how much punishment I subject myself to, it isn't enough. The shame and emptiness doesn't go away. I cry.

"Maria... I am... I'm... so... so... sorry, baby. I'd give anything to have you back."

I stop the tape.

The winter evening covers the sky in darkness. In the quiet upper-middle-class neighborhood tree lined streets are made plush by freshly manicured lawns. My residence stands dark and empty amidst its warmly lit surroundings filled with families; people together, eating, laughing, sleeping; their homes are like the diamond stars in the sky giving life to the umbra covering my street. In ignorance they live an existence they believe they created for themselves. Maybe they did, in a way. Their reality a choice from the many available. If one thing were different tonight would they be in this neighborhood eating dinner, or a homeless shelter hoping their favorite meal is on the menu? Homes live and breathe with people. My home compares to theirs with an emptiness akin to a corpse's shell.

I ease myself from the car. My body aches. I need to clean my wounds. In each miniscule move dried blood on the fabric of my clothes tears painfully from the clinging bonds of flesh made with my body. Her stench covers my face and neck making me feel sticky, sour. I deserve to feel this way. I deserve being a toilet of disgust for someone like Her to take out her frustrations. I stagger inside the house. The pain controls my movement. My guide. In tears I crumble to the floor. A voice pierces the darkness. My heart races.

"Get up! ...Get up, Adam."

My muscles prepare for fight or flight. I freeze. My senses try to rationalize the situation.

"Get up!"

He says again. My shame and anger merge. I want to get up but my pride, my ego, refuse to allow it. If anyone else asked me to rise from my position I might have given it consideration but his command incites rebellion and refusal.

"What are you doing here, Carl?"

His shadowy figure looms in the darkness of my foyer. He is not alone.

"I am here because of you. You are in great pain my friend. Your infection is spreading."

"I don't need any help!"

"Then stand up."

I wonder if this blind man knows if I am sitting or standing.

"Ok. I'm up. You happy?"

His pause eats at me. I feel ashamed for lying to him, but my anger won't allow me to acknowledge the shame.

126

"Your infection is worse than I thought. Adam, the world is full of people who have no integrity. They feel as if they can be deceptive when no one other than them defines the truth. It is probably the worst sign of infection. Men and women who do things they are ashamed of in the light, but take pleasure of under the cover of darkness are truly living in sin. Is it evil that you tell a blind man you're standing when we both know you're laying down? All you had to do was be honest, but the infection allows your thoughts to be sinister. You travel to see a woman who treats you like slime. She beats you. She degrades you. You smell of her waste. Is this what brings you pleasure now? Is this something you are proud to share with those you love? Is this something you would like to share with Maria?"

My rage boils. I leap to my feet. A smaller figure behind him runs to shield him from my potential. I scream.

"You bastard! This is all your fault. You did this to me! You did this! My face. My wife. My daughter. Everything I knew, you took away! Yes, I lied about standing up. I lied because you lied. You told me we were going to help the world with this magnificent Truth. You didn't tell me we are part of a group planning to cleanse the world of our definition of infected humans and that I'm supposed to be the great teacher who only disinfects a small number of chosen people because of their educational privileges. So please, spare me the lecture on integrity when you sound like a hypocrite."

The petite figure hovers fiercely in front of him. I think it absurd that such a little figure even conceives to stop me. As my eyes adjust I see Ms. Amen holding something shiny in her hand. It looks like a knife.

"I didn't lie to you Adam. I helped you when no one else would. I reached out my hand to you in friendship and honesty to help you fight the very thing that took you away from your family. I didn't take your face – they did! I gave you a face you could live with. Now I see I was wrong. Your brilliance prevented me from seeing your infection. What I gave you and what you gave yourself are two very different things. If I'd left you on the street you wouldn't even know you had a daughter. You wouldn't know how Maria spent her last days. You'd probably be in a laboratory underground getting probed and brainwashed but instead you stand before me now and you curse me. You defy me. You lie to me when the only thing I asked of you was to let worthy people know the Truth. That was it: one condition, one you agreed to, and this is what you bring me back. You smell of waste and death. You curse and lie to those who love you. Your perverse fetish of shame. You only answer to yourself and are better off as an infected drunk. At least you would be true to admit you're an alcoholic. Don't bother coming back to the class in the morning, we don't need you. You've done your job. I'm glad that Princess will never know you as her father, an infected addict who couldn't save himself to save anyone else. I pray you survive the Day of Judgment."

The door. I want to say something respond apologize -- anything -- nothing. Ms. Amen cautiously guarding him. In pain, I rise from the ground. She closes the door. I look out the window. They are gone.

Chapter XIV: The Monkey's Ladder

The morning sunlight invades my home. I find myself on the living room floor, an empty bottle on its side lays next to me. Well, it isn't completely empty. A swallow of liquor balances itself in the middle of the bottle. I grab it, craving the sweet taste inside. I turn the bottle upside down to devour the swallow. I need more. Stumble to the kitchen. Something smells sour. Me. I still have not showered. The waste of my Mistress mixes with the other odors of my body making my stomach turn. I suspend my search for more liquor and head to the shower.

Had last night been a dream? Had Carl and Ms. Amen really been in my home? Why would Ms. Amen act like that toward me? Am I a threat? It seemed real. The words he said apply to me. The words I said, I feel. Maybe it didn't happen. The pain and euphoria from the evening spent with my Mistress coupled with my alcoholic binge can certainly explain a delusional experience. I increase the temperature of the water, cleansing the wounds inflicted during the encounter. The steamy liquid ignites my flesh; the punishment for my taboo. Cleansing. In my delusion Carl told me not to return to work, but that's where I need to go.

How could he expect my abrupt absence to solve anything? It must have been a dream. He wouldn't make a decision like that, nor would the Dean condone such an act. I laugh. The whole recollection is absolutely absurd. It definitely gives me a reason to reconsider my choices in coping with this pain. One thing is right, Maria wouldn't want me living like this. I need to leave Mistress alone. I need to leave the alcohol alone. I don't remember drinking last night. I need help. The Dean could help. Clarity is an important thing. I need to pull myself together for Maria and our daughter. I need to give Maria's life meaning. If I give up then all they did to her will be... I can't let that happen. I shut the water off, finally feeling clean. Time to get to work.

I arrive at campus a little later than usual. I open the door to the lecture hall listening for a heated discussion, nothing. No one. I walk into the lecture hall. I need the Dean. My search ends. I open the door and there he stands.

"Dean! What's going on? Where is the class?"

He looks at me with a raised brow.

"What are you doing here?"

"What do you mean, 'what am I doing here'? I work here. This is my classroom. I told you I'd be a little late today. It hasn't been over an hour. Did you dismiss class?"

He continues looking at me as though he doesn't understand.

"Why are you looking at me like that? What is going on?"

He turns and walks toward the door. Moving around the room inspecting the chairs. He closes the entrance door to the lecture hall and locks it.

"Dean! I demand to know what is going on here!"

He puts his index finger to his lips signaling me to be quiet. He then walks to the projection screen and presses play, turning the volume all the way up. A psychology video on multiple personality disorder displays loudly. Standing in front of the screen, he motions me to come closer. We stand face to face, he places his arm around my neck, pulling me close, he whispers in my ear.

"Do you understand what this is? This is not a circus where some holy blind man and foolish Dean save the world. This is a vast network of people who don't know each other and at times don't even like each other, working together toward the purification of everything you see. You are not the only Professor and I am not the only Dean. Politicians, scientists, businessmen and women, lawyers, doctors, hippies, racists, liberalists, conservatives, taxi drivers, farmers, fishermen, police, soldiers, news reporters, etcetera are all parts of this network. We are all over the world. This is not a joke. The roles we play in society are extensive, but each of us are professors of the Truth. You are not special. You are not the only one. What we did for you, we did because we thought you wanted to help. We don't owe you anything! You're not the only one who's lost loved ones to this cause.

"My wife and son were killed after she found proof of scientific discoveries that were being suppressed by the World Health Organization. She died in a car accident on the Autobahn. When I inquired as to what happened, they told me the results of the investigation said my wife's blood alcohol was 10 times the legal limit. With my son in the car? My wife graduated top of her class in journalism. She wrote articles for some of the most prestigious media outlets in the world. After discovering the corporate greed of the media, she went into freelance journalism investigating corporate and political corruption. Through her investigations I discovered the Truth. Through understanding her work, I was able to meet Carl and the others. I followed the path. My wife never had a drink in her life. She hated alcohol!"

He took his arm from around me, pulling away at the same time. The message he whispered in my ear resonating in my thoughts. He raised his finger to his lips signaling me to remain silent. He turned the video projector off.

"You'll find your class with Mr. Clark. Now, if you'll excuse me Professor, I have some matters to attend to. I hope you find what you're looking for."

He's gone and I am alone.

Like a machine rolling taffy, my stomach churns in tightening knots. My vision disconnects from my body. My legs move, I can't feel them. I see myself moving, drawn to a destination under a power not my own. A place where my answers await. Floating. The sounds of the world around me are muffled. Are my hands over my ears? Flows of people bump against me on the afternoon sidewalk. High noon, a mass feeding of the Beast. The downtown herds move fast to nourish the beast. They hunger for the time of their lives. Emptying their pockets, they tithe to make sure the Beast is satisfied. Their hoofs beat the concrete, galloping. Other than that I can only hear the sound of my breath. I enter the hospital unaccompanied by my class. I move hastily through maze the nurses, technicians, doctors, and patients. I finally find the door. It opens with ease. He still doesn't look at me. He only stares out of his window as usual.

131

"Your class left over an hour ago."

How does he know it's me? There has to be a reflection. I run up behind him looking for a mirror before he can hide it. His hands rest on the arms of his wheelchair. He doesn't flinch. He doesn't move at all. I don't see a mirror on the walls, only his open window in front of us and a single portrait on the wall, The Last Supper. It has to be the picture; he sees me because of that image. As I grab it off the wall, he speaks,

"That's an interesting picture to put in a place full of crazy people. The Last Supper? Looks like Thanksgiving. A time when all the families, or people in general, are gathered in large groups. Even homeless. That's when they're going to do it."

I look up from my examination of the picture.

"This is when they're going to do what?"

I ask realizing he can see me without the picture.

"When they implement the next phase in our extraterrestrial evolution. Technology, space travel, immortality. A new-fangled type of human being, the alien roaming the universe – the mind invaded by a dang parasite. Human beings consume destruction and drop toxic waste; this we carve as our path.

"Holidays are supposed to be safe days where the festive mood of the season gathers us for celebration. Mass communication is a spell – a controlling influence. They influence us with broadcasted messages and we just follow those messages blindly. Most don't ever question the messenger. If it's broadcasted, it must be true. You know what I mean? They did it to you before. Remember? They called you a murderer and said you must be caught at once. That's how easily they can spark a spell. It's not some conspiracy where all sorts of media outlets are conspiring against some person or place in the world. Naww, it's a lot simpler than that. Stage, or incite a public event. Use a radical group without the group ever knowing who's behind it. That's just inspiration and Bam! You have full-fledged chaos. Now... What happens when you have chaos?"

I slide down the wall to the floor, clutching the image of The Last Supper. Looking at it, I answer him,

132

"When there's chaos... Order must be restored."

For the first time he turns toward me and I see his eyes. One hundred and fifteen years of life have passed before is grayish-blue eyes. His dark features are enhanced by the bright, penetrating color of his eyes. I drop the painting. He speaks,

"Yes... Yes... There must be order."

He wheels himself closer to me until only an inch or two separates us. Leaning down, he whispers,

"The kind of order that must be restored will not be the same order that was. A new order must be established after chaos. A new order of the Beast."

Picking up the portrait, he remarks,

"The Roman Empire sentenced a man named Jesus to die and then hundreds of years after his death and after those who knew him were long gone, they built a great church dedicated to his memory and resurrection? Ain't that crazy? Every image of him has been created by people who never laid eyes on him. No living person could validate these depictions drawn hundreds of years after his death. So, here we have an image for us to worship, but none of us, not even the people that drew it, know exactly what the image should look like. That's how easily men and women are fooled. Just like my Ma used to say, the blind lead the blind.

"Have you ever heard the story of the five monkeys?"

He chuckles.

"This is really funny. Listen. Five monkeys are placed in a cage with a ladder in the center of it. Suspended above the ladder is a bushel of bananas. The monkeys play for a while until one gets curious about the bushel. As soon as the curious monkey starts to climb the ladder toward the bananas, it gets sprayed with ice cold water. But here's the kicker, the other four monkeys in the cage get sprayed with ice cold water too. Soon another monkey decides he wants to try his luck with the bananas and goes to climb the ladder; again all five of the monkeys get sprayed with ice-cold water. This happens several times until the monkeys get wise. They figure out that as soon as one of them gets on the ladder, they're all going to get punished, so they stop trying to get the bananas."[i]

He laughs.

"Here comes the best part. One of the original monkeys is replaced with a new monkey; the new monkey sees the bananas and immediately goes to climb the ladder. When he does this, the other four monkeys pull him off the ladder and beat him up. Now, this new monkey doesn't know why he got beat up, but he doesn't want that to happen again, so he simply avoids the ladder for fear of getting attacked by the others. Again and again, original monkeys get replaced. Each time a new monkey comes in, he attempts to step on the ladder, and when he does he gets attacked by the others. This process continues until all of the original monkeys who were sprayed with the water have been replaced with monkeys who have never been sprayed."

He laughs, shaking his head,

"With all new monkeys in the cage none of them go near the ladder. They obey a rule they did not create. Not one of them got the original punishment of being sprayed by ice cold water; they simply follow a ritual without knowing the origin of why it's there. That is us. They have conditioned us like the monkeys. We obey rules we didn't make. Don't curse! Don't speak out of turn!"[ii]

He wheels himself back to the window. Still holding The Last Supper in his hand, he speaks,

"The world needs to be in chaos for a new order and world domination to begin. They're just fatten us up and keeping us dependent. Those who are independent must be neutralized and reformed. This is what the Beast commands of us."

I sit, absorbing his words. The indoctrination of humanity in the simple story of monkeys and a ladder consumes my thinking. The ladder representing freedom, the ability to explore the world around us, the freedom to enjoy the things within our reach; the bananas, the motivation to strive for something we naturally desire. Once upon a time, this was the essence of humanity. Now we are twisted. The monkeys' fear overruled their natural desire to reach beyond their unnatural confines into something right and real — the reward of eating bananas. Fear controls them just as it controls us. The original group held back the new who had never been sprayed. The new monkeys represent a new generation: the infant, the baby, our children. We hold back our newly born with our inculcations. We force them to adhere to rules and standards oppressing their natural desires and abilities. We do this having never been sprayed ourselves. We oppress our children into the system. We make them believe in the Tooth Fairy, Easter Bunny, etcetera, things we were taught to believe in. We believe blindly, or accept beliefs into our lives for fear of punishment by our peers, or society at large. If we challenge the other monkeys by trying to climb the ladder, we will be attacked. So instead of challenging we assimilate to ways and customs we don't like for fear going against popular opinion. He speaks,

"You can see world domination in the leashes we wear, in our tribute to the Beast. Think about it. Why do we wear neckties and bowties? In a world full of fashion trends, why is that fashion still a form of status and respect associated with men in business? Recognized worldwide, ways of dress and customs once unique to a region as symbols of power are replaced with a universally recognized symbol: the suit and tie. Every freakin' country in the world recognizes this as a symbol of status. Why? They don't know. You don't know. We just do it. We just accept it. We refuse to climb the ladder to grab the bananas because we are afraid. What happens to a powerful man who refuses to wear a suit and tie? He's attacked as unprofessional. The judgments from the public are broadcast until he finds himself dragged down the platform as a symbol for those who try to follow in his footsteps. This is how you can see it. Watch the world news and look at the people who follow the order and those who rebel against it. The ones who don't wear the uniform of the Beast are neutralized and attacked. Now that's world order."

He turns to me lifting the picture from his lap, but this time it looks different, like a feast of poison. He speaks,

"You see, the cleansing goes both ways. No matter who wins we find ourselves at The Last Supper. That is the answer for you. It is time you find your class."

He places the picture face down on his lap and turns back toward his window. The door opens the mousey nurse informs me it is time to leave, Mr. Clark needs to take his medication.

Walking through the hallways of the hospital I'm greeted by familiar faces. I think I see Ms. Emch. I think I see Mr. LaDay wearing a doctor's coat. I reach for him, but I am wrong; they look alike, but the man doesn't know me. The encounters with Carl, the Dean, Ms. Amen, and Bug have warped my perceptions. The ladder. We are afraid to step on the ladder. My students need to know. There will be a cleansing of the earth and there's nothing we can do to avoid it. There is no middle ground. One species becomes extinct; another species flourishes: the cycle of life's energy. I am immersed in the world of appearances.

Chapter XV: The Key

A folded note rests in my pocket, my name scrawled across the outside. I don't know how the paper got in my pocket. Leaving the hospital I reach for my keys and find it. It reads, *Go to Willows Park*.

Here I am, directed by a note from an unknown source standing in Willows Park. The wind blows soft and crisp, whistling through the trees.

"Psssst!"

I turn toward the noise.

"Psssst!"

Hiding on the side of a willow tree peeking at me is Ms. Amen. She motions to come to her. I hesitate; our last encounter left me leery of her intentions. Did she put the note in my pocket? With reservations I begin to walk. She doesn't look like the innocent deaf girl I first met in class. She looks cold, callous. I enter her reach and she grabs me putting her finger to my lips.

"Shhhh...."

She looks at me smiling hard, almost laughing. She covers her mouth with one hand and with the other she points beyond a thicket of bushes next to the tree where we crouch. It is my class. I stand to see them, but she pulls me down shaking her head.

"Why? I want to tell them. They need to know..."

"Shhhh...." She insists.

"Did you write the note?"

She shakes her head no.

"Who wrote the note?"

"I wrote the note."

A familiar voice emanates behind me. The bass tones reverberate through my chest. Slowly, I turn around. My eyes well up with tears. Redemption. Relief. My cause. My mission. My work. My words, better left to silence, come out in gasps for breaths.

"My ignorance. My arrogance. My ego. I shouldn't have done the things I did."

I close my eyes to change reality. Praying for an awakening from this nightmare. Forgiveness, grant sleep to wake from my dreams.

"There is nothing for you to be ashamed of, or sorry for. We all must make our way in the darkness toward enlightenment." He says.

The newborn day comes to my dreams. I open my eyes to look up at him with infant like vision blurred by my tears.

"Thank you for your forgiveness."

"Forgiveness? I have not been in a place of forgiveness in many years. In order to forgive, there must be some sort of resentment. I do not resent you. The infection within you is not something I can pass judgment for or against. Like any other disease, it is something you must deal with in your own space. I cannot, nor can anyone else, judge a disease you've been afflicted by. What you suffer is part of your existence. I feel no indignation toward you, because you have done nothing to me. What you have done, you have done to yourself. My place is here not inside you."

He kneels to sit before me.

"You are a Professor of Truth. Your job is more important than any. This journey that has only just begun. Your infection is not a curable disease. You must live with it and live past it. You make this journey on your own. This process must run its natural course so that you can achieve the freedom to continue."

He rises from his place to stand in the face of gravity. Everything is spinning around us. I know what's coming. In this moment I wish I could stop time and never allow it to move forward again. I would hold this moment forever because I can never get this moment back.

"I do not have the power to take your job from you. No one can take your job from you. It is something that lives inside you; it is something for you to treasure. Keep the key I gave you close to your heart. It will open a door of many answers someday, but you can only use it once and only when it's time; you will feel it and use it to understand."

"What about my class?"

He grabs his walking stick.

"You have been identified by the largest Protectors. See your students at your own risk."

"Wait! What about the Dean's work? What about our work? I thought there'd be another class?"

He smiles.

"There will always be a class. You and the students will continue."

"What will the students think? How will the class go on without me?"

He puts his hand on my shoulder.

"The students have been instructed to continue with their studies. Ms. Amen will guide them with your notes."

"How will I find her?"

He shakes his head.

"You won't. She will find you. I must be going, my friend. I want you to be very careful. There is a war going on, a war we don't see, waged against the people. You are a part of this struggle as a registered malcontent for anarchy. Be careful my friend. They will do whatever they can to destroy you. Teach wherever you find those receptive to the lesson. Look to your class."

Through the bushes I see Ms. Amen making her way back to the group. They are sitting in a circle talking, laughing, and enjoying each other's company. Instead of learning with them, sharing with them, experiencing with them, I watch. How many of us have played this part? Not a participant; the person ineligible to play. How many of us have watched and done nothing, looking at the world, trapped in our own perspective? What do you see?

"Carl, why do people watch the world around them instead of living, sharing, experiencing, and participating? It doesn't make sense. If we were more active, could we be saved? Could this Beast we created be stopped?"

He is gone.

It has to be here. I couldn't have put it anywhere else. I made sure to put it in a safe place. I taped it underneath a drawer in my dresser. The tape remained where I put it, but the key had been removed. The key he gave me when I embarked on this journey, I cannot find it. How would I know what to do when the time came to use it, if I cannot find it? My house is in disarray. Maybe I moved it from beneath the drawer. What have I done? The key might lead to my daughter. He told me to keep it close to my heart and when the time came I'd understand. What could be closer to my heart than Maria and our daughter? I owe Maria my life. I owe our daughter my life. I rip my house to shreds looking for the key, searching every inch of my home until there is nothing left to explore. I tear through letters and books, through every piece of garbage in every basket, through each container in my house, under and behind every piece of furniture. I dismantle the hutch in my dining room. I take the tires off of my car. I rip the fabric off my couches and destroy my mattress. I cannot find the key.

My daughter, my wife, my class, the danger my existence places on people. I can no longer remain at this home. Again I have to run for my life and I don't want to create a new one. I cannot find the key.

The television blares loudly in the cheap and filthy motel room. I turn it up as loud as it can go. I made sure no one was staying in either of the rooms next to me. No one knows I am here. The time has come to issue the final assignment to the students. I want to see them, but it is too dangerous. They must carry on the message. The full Truth, they have to discover on their own. As they continue their lives, the lessons here will lay in the back of their minds. The lesson of my life and the truth of my death will serve as a reminder to always be aware of the big picture. There's more to life than what they see and know. The final assignment will be to define the direction of human existence and the basis for this direction. I hope they will tone down the human need for over explanation. I want them to condense their thoughts into pure essential thinking: no elaboration, just simple and direct. Convey your message of understanding and perspective in as few words as possible. Describe the images you envision.

The tail end of the noose around my neck is slung over my shoulder as I finish the message; I can't wait to tie it to the ceiling fan above. Soon I'll be with my beloved.

I lick the envelope containing the final assignment; the Dean's name is on the front.

The television blares breaking news, a volcanic eruption has wiped out a small village. The center of the Earth holds our core essence. They figured out long ago how to create life for us on any planet using a planet's core as a catalyst. The special liquid that flows to the center of our planet delves deep where the planet's dreams are in their purest form. New creatures, new life, new world. Who knows the truth? A planet's dreams come alive in water.

I secure the end of the rope to the ceiling fan. Tightening the noose around my neck I say a prayer for my daughter, "May she know my love for her and may we one day be united. I love you Nancy."

I close my eyes tight and kick the chair from under my feet. The rope tightens around my neck like a ripcord. The burn of the rope's grip sears my flesh. I choke and gurgle as my body fights to stay alive. The struggle to live is involuntary. My body fights, but slowly gives in to the inevitable. Acceptance takes over the resistance. A peace begins to come over me. Is this what Maria felt?

The door bursts open and I struggle to look as my body loses its life. A woman's silhouette stands in the doorway. The fog of death is claiming my vision. The figure rushes towards me. I catch a glimpse of her face. ...Maria?

The ritual of impending death has a procedure when the system is notified, the trek of a life rescued in a civilized world: flashing lights and the sounds of energetic people doing all they can to help the body sustain life. The noise. The sirens. Flirting with consciousness. Images flash before opening and closing eyes. Only in my review can I put the images together to understand how my life was saved. The ritual of impending human death.

I am not a religious person, but I do believe in a higher power. Something is responsible for this. How did this happen? I want to end my life and this system won't let me do it. The intervention could be

141

considered divine. Hanging from a rope only seconds from death, the powers that be snatching me from the rope and saving my life. My life? My life? Who, what, can be so arrogant as to give me life when I no longer want to live? Divine intervention or divine ownership? Some condemn me for my actions. They give me a second chance. A second chance at what? This world, full of magical powers, bombs that drop out of the sky from unmanned planes, and trips off our planet to lunar colonies and space stations. We communicate with devices that cannot be seen. Aliens. We still think we are not aliens? Look up the word. We are not of this nature. We have created another world out of this one, with no sovereign place to go back to. Cast out. The majority of us would die naked in the wilderness. Our feet are too soft to walk without shoes. The city hunt; bargain shopping. We spend. We slaughter. We waste. We take all natural things of this Earth and make them unnatural with chemicals and synthetics. Even our food has become unnatural with additives and preservatives. Our stomachs cannot drink unpurified water; natural freshwater has the power to kill us. We live like a foreign substance of this world carrying with us pollution and toxic waste. We exist as parasites building a poisonous colony inside of a monster that feasts on the planet. Nothing divine can be found in this. The belly of the Beast landed on this planet long ago.

When I was in college the origins of earthly life were a mystery. Theory upon theory proposing the origin of life on Earth have been argued and studied. We can apply traits and laws to experiments, but no scientist could create life from thin air. Most scientists believe that a great series of events spanning billions of years throughout many different conditions which could never be duplicated in a laboratory created life in the universe. Some call the beginning of this a divine event The Big Bang Theory. Others aren't so sure. Maria and I rest among those who are not so sure.

We published a theory of the universe called, "The Big Bang, Bang, Bang" which stated simply, "The universe never began. It has and will always exist in one form or another. As human beings, it is too difficult for us to understand something that has no ending and no beginning.

142

In our simple minds, everything must have a start and an end, the reason for the Big Bang Theory. The universe is expanding from this bang and will someday collapse on itself. How is that possible? If the universe is expanding, what lay outside of its expansion? What is the universe expanding inside of? If the universe is not infinite then there is something outside of the universe's expansion that is infinite, there is infinity in the process of inner and outer things. Meaning, there is a double mirror effect of continuous duplication; thus, we are the smallest and largest thing in the duplication making us infinite and all realities possible. Anything you imagine can exist.

"If we use the big bang theory, then we must establish how the universe began. Its expansion is either a constant or repeating event. If it is constant, then we don't understand it. If it is a repeating event, expansion and collapse, then we are in a never ending evolutionary process. What exists in the vacated space after collapse?"

Our theory shook our colleagues. Many older scientists scolded us for the radical theory. Some said we were trying to introduce religion into the science community with implications of the divine presence outside our existence and understanding. If a divine presence exists, then it exists as if it doesn't, and inside our understanding it's the existence of a theory with its only proofs as debatable phenomena. The big bang, bang, bang. God, a microscopic enormity – the smallest and largest as one.

As I lay in my hospital bed hooked up to machines meant to keep me alive, I still wish I was no longer living. Reflecting the path to my present moment is painful. She is gone, lost on a journey we began together. I miss her. The sedative begins to take effect and sleep finds me once again.

She stands above me. I cannot move. Her face is covered by shadows. I lay on my back in paralysis. Her boots are familiar though Her face is obscured. Mistress. My body braced for pain. I want to tell Her to go away. I try to speak. The sound from my body is gone. I try to scream out in frustration using all the force and energy I contain. Nothing, no sound escapes from me. Can she possibly see my effort? I hope she doesn't. She stands over me, one leg on either side of my body. I don't want to see her anymore. There is nothing I can do. I brace for her painful touch and close my eyes. She speaks,

"Beep... Beep... Beep... Beep."

A machine? She's a machine? I can hear Her breath in between the beeps, and feel it close to my face. I can feel her. My heart races. Her breathing begins to race too. I fear her power and intention to hurt me. Her torturous delay holds me captive in anticipation of what I know to be inevitable: the sting of Her touch. Goosebumps float on the naked parts of my skin. She is getting closer. My breath becomes short and fast as she draws near.

"Beep, beep, beep, beep – beep, beep."

She touched me, freeing me from my paralysis. I jump up and open my eyes, awakening from a dream. I'm still in a hospital bed but Ms. Amen is standing next to me, with her hand outstretched, holding in her palm, a key. The key. My key. The one I'd been missing.

Chapter XVI: Goodbye

The revelation to leave came in the form of an advertisement for laundry detergent. I already questioned my ability to be effective in my current position in this place so far from everything I'd ever known. In my wildest dreams I never pictured life like this, scars on my chest from cigarette burns, scars from the lashes of her whip, my neck decorated by the marks from my noose. I lay in the hospital bed, a victim of my own villain's ways. The woman I love, dead. My daughter, missing, possibly forever. The class... The advertisement...

If you'd like to get away, then make a clean start. Wash yesterday away and start clean ...today.

The words speak directly to me. The direction, heaven sent. Leave and start over. I had been given the key. I needed to speak with a few people before departure. I need to make sure the students understand their final lesson.

I leave the hospital in search of my disciples. I know which one to contact first. The easiest to find and the first in the class. His awareness essential to the success of this mission.

The football field on the college campus stands virtually empty this time of year. A champion's field abandoned to the few who use the track and wannabes playing catch, none here now match up to those who won on the same battle ground. It made the emptiness of the field stand great. A lone gladiator stood on the field running routes as if his team and fans in the arena. Watching him practice I can hear and see what he must imagine: the stadium filled with fans and teammates cheering him to victory. I see why he is so great at his craft. What an amazing disciple he will be. The future champion wide receiver of a professional football team, they'd never suspect him as knowing the Truth.

Seeing me approach he shifts his focus.

"Professor? Professor... Hey I can't believe it's you. How are you?"

"Yes, Mr. Macpherson it's me. I'm fine."

"Professor, we thought you'd quit. The Dean told us you were ill and probably wouldn't be back to class before the semester ended. He said you would send us our final assignment and the class would be over. It was disappointing to think that we wouldn't be seeing you again... We... We were worried. Are you coming back to finish teaching the class?"

I pause to appreciate his genuine concern. Even now as I reflect while listening to the recordings of my mind, I can close my eyes and see the concern on his face. My students. My effect on them has meaning.

"No, Mr. Macpherson, I will not be coming back to class."

"Is everything okay?"

"Yes, everything is okay. It's time for a change. I have to be moving on."

"Why?"

"That's not important. What is important is the class."

"The class? I'm not sure I understand Professor. Do you mean the subject of the class?"

"No, the meaning of our study. Why did we do this course? This entry into the truth of reality initiates a belief. Perception. There is so much more for you to learn. Are you ready?"

"Professor... What you talking about? Are you ok? "

Hearing that I wonder if I have made the right choice in coming. Maybe I should've just gone clean like the advertisement said. I studied his eyes, trying to see if I'd made the correct decision. He wants to be free. He just probably doesn't understand freedom lives inside the core of a being's perceptions of belief. His mind is protectively skeptical, but curious. An open mind.

"I cannot be here long. What I have to tell you is important. Let's go sit somewhere and talk."

I steer us towards the shaded parts of the arena. We take our places fifteen rows up from the field under the first deck. Once we are seated, I begin.

"Mr. Macpherson, this world is not as we'd like to make it. Our limited view keeps us locked in a reality we think we know, but really we don't grasp our place in space. Take the stadium. Long ago stadiums provided entertainment for games beyond friendly competition. Over two thousand years ago, this type of setting provided us with true blood sport."

"Yes, Professor I know. I am aware of ancient western civilization."

"Okay, that's good. Since you are aware, then you must understand this establishment is ancient?"

"Yes, Professor."

"Then, in knowing that you must understand your place in this ancient activity? You are not in something you created, but inside of something someone else created, and that simply knowing this your place is not important in continuing, or maintaining this ancient process. You merely fill a place in the scheme. Do you understand what that means to your day to day activity? We see the moment, but not the moment's place."

A mind is opening to the infinite possibilities of the universe, a small but significant opening in a wall of teachings created to block out independent thought.

"Professor, I do understand that my role in society is one that needs to be filled, and if I do not fill the position it will be filled by someone else. I do not end or begin the acts of society. It was created before me and it continues independent of the individual but, Professor... That does not make my role or my existence insignificant to the process. My actions are mine to express the definition of the role's identity of participation, and thus different from others who may do the same."

I smile at his attempt to protect the wall built for him, his shot to close the opening.

"No," I say, "no, it doesn't make your position or your existence insignificant. As individuals, we are all important. As with pieces to a puzzle, every piece fits to complete the picture. A puzzle with a missing piece leaves the picture incomplete. Everyone means something."

I smile.

"Mr. Macpherson, I am asking you to grasp another realm of consciousness and go to a place where beings *truly* live. Right now, we are not in that place. The picture of this puzzle has been designed by people with an agenda that most cannot even comprehend. The picture they've seen fit to create, and the one we see as pieces are not the same. Pieces don't see the complete picture as they simply participate in the grand scheme of connections, fitting where they are supposed to go. We don't see the picture until the puzzle is complete. These ancient processes we participate in have been established to put this puzzle together and we play our parts connecting the dots of this ugly picture, Mr. Macpherson. Do you see the image we are creating?"

An obvious change in his expression. Anxious for his response, I waited in the agony of possible failure or success. The type of agony a gambler goes through when the dice are rolling with all the chips bet. Hoping... Hoping... Hoping the wager pays off. He says,

"I see what you mean about the grand scheme of things and us being pieces to a puzzle. I've been thinking a lot since our study of Ms. Rivera."

"Interesting. How have you been thinking about her?"

"Our sessions with Ms. Rivera were unlike anything I've ever experienced in a class. You have to admit we have a cool class. Our lectures, our labs, our study... how many people get graded credit in school for their own experiences? Most classes are text and test based. To get credit for having independent thought is refreshingly cool. We're not being forced to learn, or threatened by failure through bad grades. Just by thinking about the things we studied, we pass the course. Even the message in my notes, *We don't know anything*, I told my coach about it. After a game one day he started tearing into our asses about not learning the playbook. When Coach gets mad, his veins start pulsing, you know? He gets real serious when it comes to football. When he's done I asked if he had a minute. He was still kind of mad, breathing real hard; if anybody else would've asked him he would've ripped them a new one but it's me, so he said okay. We go to his office and I blurt out straight to the point. We are studying some intense psychiatric patients. Coach knows I'm into the psychology thing. He's like a dad to me. I tell him everything about how I'm feeling, you know? Coach has been there for me since I got here. I spend holidays at his house with him and his wife. They don't have any kids, I think that's why Coach is always on us like he is. Anyway, when he gets too worked up yelling, it calms him down to talk about my classes. So we get to talking about the patients and he asks me what my assignments and projects are like. I tell him there are no assignments or projects. Coach looks at me like I'm crazy or something and then says,

"'How are you doing on the tests?'

"I laugh and tell him we don't have tests.

"'You don't have any tests?' He says in his gruff voice, 'How the hell are you learning?'

"It is hilarious because Coach can't understand how I am learning in a class without tests or projects. That's when I tell him about the heading in my notes. *We don't know anything*. He told me I was right and we started laughing. He said,

'I can see you're enjoying your class with no work, it looks good on you.'

His face always looks like he's mad but he smiles in his best nice way. I told him, 'It's not work, it's experience.'

"I used to believe the heading in my notes was a question, *We don't know anything?* That question, it challenged me. It called me out like another football team coming to our school, *our* house for a game. How dare they? I told Coach, just like I'm telling you now, and it still gets me pumped up. The nerve of that heading to tell me I don't know anything. Where the hell does that heading in my notes get off telling me I don't know anything? I'm Wesley Macpherson, star wide receiver for the number one college football team in the country. My name has been in local and national sports pages every Friday, Saturday, Sunday, Monday and sometimes Tuesday. Do you hear me Professor? I'm one of the greatest college football players that has ever lived. Where does that heading in my notes get off telling me I don't know anything? So I start thinking about the things I know and start wondering how I know these things. Are these things I know important to me as a person, or as someone who has to fit a certain place to play a certain role in this society? The heading in my notes started to really trip me out. I began to push my mind and think about thinking. I thought about what I know and what it's for. Those things I know make sense for society, but what about for me? My being? I told Coach I didn't understand the purpose for the things I know. Coach isn't the type of guy who shows weakness, he believes showing feelings other than anger is a sign of weakness. He could see how complex this dilemma had grown in my mind. He said,

"'The things you know are for your survival. Only the strong survive. That's why you know what you know. You learn what you need to survive. You make a choice to learn what serves you best.'

"My survival? My knowledge is for my survival? My knowledge makes me strong and so I survive? How could the things I know make so little sense to me and yet make so much sense to the world? My knowledge of football could someday take care of me. The more I know about football, the stronger I become. What is football? Football only means something to those who think about it. The power of belief. Our first lecture with the great Professor: the power of belief.

"What we believe as a collective becomes that much greater. Ms. Rivera said that money is not real but all of us accept it and recognize its power. We fall into a belief system we didn't create. In our first class you told us there is nothing stronger we can challenge than a person's beliefs, or our own beliefs. For centuries people have died over beliefs. It's a powerful thing to challenge. So my belief is part of my survival? No! My survival is irrelevant. The group always prevails. Individually, within a system, our lives are to play a role. We take part in a show, a production. It doesn't matter who plays the part or how good or bad the acting is. The show is written and so by popular opinion, it is performed. We are performers for a play we did not write but our independent acts bring it to life. Our independent thoughts are absorbed by the group. It's not about me. Beliefs are about us.

"I told Coach Mr. Clark's story, the one about the cage with the monkeys and the ladder. The scientists indoctrinated the original monkeys and the original monkeys indoctrinated the next generation of monkeys. I told him that is how we perform in this play of society. Generation after generation of 'this is how things are supposed to be and don't ask any questions,' is passed down generation to generation.

"When I told Coach that, he looked at me with the only emotion I'd ever seen him display – anger. He said this class has my head in the clouds and I need to stop thinking like a hippie and start thinking like a man. I had to ask him... What is a man and what is a hippie? His nostrils flared like a bull out of breath, his words were explosive and fast, hitting as if he held a weapon aimed directly at my mind. He said,

"'A man knows what he's supposed to do and a hippie's trying to figure it out. Stop acting like a hippie and start acting like a responsible man. There's no need for questions anymore. You need to have answers. What kind of man doesn't have answers for his own life? You know why you're here. You know what you're supposed to do. There's no need to be thinking about anything else. We live as we do and we deal with it. You're part of the group, like a team, and this is the way the team wants to go. If you go against the team, then you become an opponent, so why question the group? You know your role. You know your position. Play your part! It doesn't matter why you can't grab the banana or go onto the ladder, just don't do it.'"

I can see Mr. Macpherson's pain, recounting the moments with his coach, he looks off into the distance of the stadium, toward the end zone where many of his battles had been won. Taking a deep breath, resolves sets in his eyes, a protective shield repressing his pain. He composes himself to continue.

"Coach used his words to redirect my thinking. It worked. I thought all I need to do was obey. As long as I obey I will be okay. My survival is close to my acceptance. I told him he was right and I was thankful for his help. He put his hand on my shoulder and said,

151

"'College can be a confusing time for a young man. Don't worry about nonsense. Do the best you can and graduate. That's all that matters in college.'

"I thanked Coach for his help and left."

Mr. Macpherson sits with glassy eyes in the battle to suppress his essence of being. The conflict, the struggle, to accept his role define by his beloved coach. He submitted to the "team". The weapon of words, the final assault of killing free thoughts. Like many in this world, he is suppressed by the group under a pressure that makes him surrender. His tears tell a deep, ancient story. In his essence the nagging, aching conflict with consciousness morally pulls away at his perception of the things around him. The talk with his coach, an example of the struggle humans face in pressure from peers. He continues,

"After talking with Coach about the class I did what I always do, I started to get ready for the next season. Intense training. With the class on break I began preparing for the final battle of my college career. I still wrestled with the thoughts introduced by our sessions. They left an impression, but football had to take top priority. We won the championship. All my energy went into the game. Then, the season ended. We won! Pro teams called. My agent, my friends, everyone gave me praise, but it wasn't enough to satisfy me. It's funny Professor... again I found myself wrestling with the thoughts from the heading in my notes and I didn't feel resolution after talking to Coach, the heading haunted me. What did it do to my beliefs? I tried to rationalize it, but rationalizing didn't give me any satisfying answers. Questions danced in my mind, puzzling me. Again ideas began to challenge my thinking, my beliefs. So when football is gone, what do I have? My escape from old thoughts I found in class. My escape from new thoughts, I found on the field. That's why when I wasn't in class I'd be here. Most people think it's because I'm the best, or I'm pushing to be the best. Naw... I wish it was that easy. I'm not here because I'm the best; I'm here because it's all I know. If I'm not here, then the reality that confronts me is one I'm not sure I want to face. Who am I? I don't want to think about that question. I can't answer who I am not being me. That means I don't know."

152

The young football player stands over 6 feet and weighs over 200 pounds. Like a lawnmower cutting grass he could easily take down a man my size. This young human male, formidable in stature, reduced to vulnerability by his own thinking. His physique is nothing compared to the power of his mind; his ideas, now closer to the center of his being.

I place my hand on his shoulder.

"What you feel is the essence of your being. What you sense and what you've been taught to believe cannot co-exist. You cannot answer the questions in your mind because it's out of character with your role. Face the truth of the creation around you. The true answer is too much for your role to bear. It's easier to simply go with what you've been taught, to believe the group than go against it. The design for this formula I call socially applied energy.

"Socially applied energy directs masses of people with a reinforced belief of the subject, cause, or object. A subject would be prayer in school or abortion. These subjects can blend into causes for some people, but they are not to be confused with a cause. Subjects are debatable and are dependent on change in social consciousness. We debate subjects. Causes are different. A cause drives you and consumes you to put forth effort regarding something you believe. Objects such as money or jewelry can hold untold power over the human mind. Animals display this sort of behavior over food or territory. We have this same basic instinct, but our instincts have been warped to focus on unnatural things. We believe in things that are alien to our nature.

"Socially applied energy speaks to the ladder in the story of the monkeys and bananas. This concept imposes preexisting beliefs upon new generations. Our natural instincts conflict with some of the ideas we are conditioned to believe. They want to eat bananas, but can't touch the ladder to get to them because their peers say touching the ladder is unlawful. An internal conflict arises because these concepts are so foreign to natural beliefs and instincts. We seek these objects, causes, and subjects placed before us by the largest Protectors. We become confused about our individual goals when we obtain the very

153

things we seek. Our ideas are not our own inceptions, but we believe them to be; this belief causes us to feel unfulfilled when we reach the attainment of predesigned desires. We obtain the abnormal things we seek and those things do not make us happy. That's where the human mind reaches the height of confusion. The world around us doesn't make sense to our internal being. We strive and strive and finally reach our goal... then there's no satisfaction to our nature. The rest of our desires become questionable. You see, humans need something to do. The thrill of the hunt consumes time, mental capacity and purpose. Though this society, which is alien to the natural human state, gives a hunt substituted with a synthetic subject, object, or cause, the misdirected search leaves us unsatisfied because it's not what our spirit's highest self truly seeks."

"What do we want Professor? What is it that we want if the things we're being shown aren't it? Is everything we know false, or is it deeper than that?"

Human emotion, our ability to grasp and comprehend from the external to the internal. Through understanding our feelings, we are able to communicate experiences to our spirit. His tears continued as he struggled to understand. Emotion on the brink of revelation grips his essence. The answer is before him.

"Our purpose is to build a different Beast. The Beast that we sustain and build now takes our essence and gives us nothing in return for our service to it. It uses our thoughts to grow stronger and gives us nothing back. The Beast we have to build is one which rewards us for our work. Not some of us, not most of us, *all of us* need to be rewarded. All of our sacrifices and all of our efforts should be equally important. Socially applied energy can be for the good of us all if used correctly.

"Instead of the monkeys keeping each other off the ladder, they all need to escape from the cage and live in a world full of banana trees. They can share their bounty and develop relationships where the sharing of their resources is natural. You see Wesley, that's how evil the cage and ladder are. How many of you in the class truly understood that fact? We all analyzed the story and felt the

154

comparison in our own existence, but how many of us understood the depth of that evil? We hurt for the monkey denied the banana, but how many of us thought the monkeys shouldn't even be in the cage? That's the problem. Monkeys shouldn't be in cages, bananas shouldn't be dangled from ropes. That is abnormal.

"Playing a role in a movie offers great wealth while working in a field harvesting food from the Earth offers little money at all. All of the importance is placed in the hands of a market of stocks that exists from a plug in the wall. Men and women who shuffle papers are rewarded as kings and queens while the people who labor are treated as fools. Vast wealth is spent on items no bigger than the palm of my hand while children starve. People put so much pressure on other people's existence. They see no other choice but to take from another. All of the rewarding knowledge is kept from the masses and given to the few. The ignorant are controlled by their ignorance. This process is ancient. This process is not our purpose. The secrets of the world are kept and held by the few. Instead of a world united by enlightened people, we have a world divided by greed and ignorance. Desperation transforms into evil. Society holds no responsibility for breeding wrong doing. People commit crimes against each other motivated by greed, desperation, frustration, or hate, and this is no fault of our own? Children are raised to rob, steal, hurt and cheat others. A child is not born knowing how to do those things. What is the reason for this?"

"...I – I don't know, Professor."

"Yes you do. You know why, it's not hard. Think about what I said. Why does a hungry child learn to rob, cheat, and steal? Why?"

"I – I don't know, Professor."

"Yes you do! Answer the question."

"Professor.... I – I can't."

"Yes you can. Think about nature. Think about predator versus prey. The hungry hyena will risk death to steal food from the lion. Think about it, answer the question: Why does the child learn to rob, steal, and cheat?"

His eyes glowed with revelation. The spark of a thought, an idea born in the mind. I watch the fire grow.

"The hyena steals from the lion out of desperation. Desperation is not taught, it is instinctual. When faced with few choices, a person must choose to live or die. If the child is hungry and she sees food, the child will do whatever she needs to do in order to obtain the food. This is not taught to the child, Professor. This is a natural instinct of desperation. The child is trying to survive."

I fueled the flame.

"Okay, then in today's time of penalty and punishment, has desperation been transformed into evil? Or has desperation always been evil?"

"I'm not sure I get what you mean, Professor?"

"Think about it, has desperation been confused with evil?"

His confusion is replaced by a glimpse of the entire picture.

"Desperation has been... I – I don't think I can really explain this properly, Professor. Evil is too complex, but we do punish people for desperate measures. People commit crimes of desperation and we don't seek to fix why. A violation has been committed and violations of the law must be punished or we have no standards to obey. Without laws in place, the system would fall apart. People taking without penalty. People violated for their possessions. Hyenas and lions running wild in open lawlessness. It's sad to think of the desperation in the hungry child, but we cannot pardon the child with forgiveness because as a society we will descend the slippery slope into lawlessness."

I smile at his perfect answer to my imperfect question. The standards of public opinion echo heavily in his voice; his answer could be a sound-bite on a news interview. Another imperfect question to further fan the flame.

"Mr. Macpherson,"

"Yes, Professor?"

"Do we punish a desperate society? Or do we punish desperate individuals?"

He offers his answer to my slithery words.

"We punish individuals, Professor. Desperate or not, we punish individuals. A violator of the law is a violator of the law. The justice system in this country is blind and only deals with the state of guilt or innocence. Yes, we do have injustice and the system is not perfect. Many innocent men and women are punished for violations of the law that they did not commit. We could debate the perfection of the justice system all night and we'd both have some really good points, but for this scenario we need not debate the merits of punishment versus justice. The sufficient answer is that we punish individuals who violate the law. The standard of justice keeps the moral fabric of our system in place. Children, adults, both genders, everyone, anyone, who violates the law must be punished. The system isn't perfect, but it's meant to be. "

It is time for him to confront his perfect answers.

"Okay... We punish individuals no matter what, for their violations of the law. So, is there is no room to understand desperation or the causes for desperation? Should we only determine guilt or innocence by of the violation of law? Sometimes our determination of justice is not correct, but the punishment is a deterrent from the violation... So, punishment dissuades violation? No... You didn't say that. You said we must punish those who violate the law, no matter who they are and that is what holds the fabric of our system together, because without that, we would have lawlessness. Okay. Okay. That seems about right. Punishment for violations of laws keep us from lawlessness and chaos. Okay... I - I have one last question for you. This one is big. Here we go.

"What good is a system with laws that are broken every day? What is society doing to correct the flaws in our system that promote desperation? We have laws in place to keep order, yet laws are broken everyday by all kinds of people. Is order broken? Is justice blind when every demographic of person has at least one who's violated some law, no matter how big or small? A system of laws which get broken everyday by every type of person. Why can't we create a system without crime? Don't answer that. That is not my question. We do need to understand that, but that is not the question I want to ask.

"Are we living in a system where laws are meant to code our morals and ethical standards, or are we in a system that has rules in place to deter most, but not all? Don't answer that. That is not my question. We do need to understand that, but that is not my question.

"My question is: What would our world be without law? Without being punished by law for our infractions, what would our world be? Where would human existence be without law?"

This final dose would either drown out the flames or breathe life into the fire. He looked into my eyes. I can feel the connection in our humanity. A hallucinating connection forms with an intoxicating effect, an out of body experience; I see the world through his eyes and grant the connection formed with sight, sound and taste of smell. The science of life forming... We see. The moments to come, the moments of the past merge into one, we understand. This powerful energy of all things exists simply in a moment of life. A shared understanding makes us one. I understand me as I understand you. Feel without physical touch. No heart-to-heart talks, no bonding rituals, just true, human connection. We share a connection most in this time will never share with another human being. We smile. He talks,

"Without law, human existence would be free to govern itself. The shift from societal law to natural law should be chaos. If different, I'd be surprised. We might be afraid of what freedom truly is because we have never lived free. Our existence and our understanding have been held, restricted, by belief. All we know is the protection of the established rules. The rules made to protect us from the evil we fear. Yet it doesn't stop evil from happening to us. The rules are imaginary but our belief in them makes them real, that is what makes them exist. We participate in a play already in progress because the play is all we know. Our fear of the unknown keeps us locked in our established roles. We are born looking for somewhere to fit in. We find a part and assimilate into the system. The law contains us and when something in our system needs to be protected, the law steps in to correct the problem. Like the monkeys, we participate in the design without personally knowing who established it. We only know the penalty of infraction. We don't think of living outside of the cage because we don't know what exists outside it. Fear of the unknown. We explore only as far as our fears allow. We have no idea what paradise could await. The foreboding feeling of losing all we know traps us inside a cage of preserved understanding. Our understanding is limited by what we choose to believe, yet our fears are drenched in the capacity of our wildest imaginations. Like imagining almost certain death if we leave the familiarity of our cage. What we don't understand can kill us, but what we fail to realize is that we don't need a pre-designed system to exist -- just like the monkeys in the cage don't need the pre-designed cage to have bananas. You know what, Professor?"

I smile.

"I don't think the monkeys are as foolish as we are. I truly believe the monkeys would flee the cage at the first opportunity and probably find a place much better to exist."

We laugh together.

"Yes, I think the monkeys would probably do much better than us."

That day I told Mr. Macpherson that he successfully completed my class. I wished him luck in his life and assured him we'd see each other again. The spark had been ignited in him. He understood our purpose. His presence would be felt in our war against the Beast. I left the stadium wondering when I'd be in his presence again. I hoped it would be sooner than later.

Chapter XVII: The Theater

The theater's capacity exceeded 3,000 seats. Its walls, floor, and ceiling; its stage, and its sunken orchestra space, and all of its seats from the floor to the balcony all hold centuries of human experiences. A smell, older than the breath in my body wafts through my senses; a fragrance constantly evolving from the odors absorbed during each event. Sounds made over centuries permeate the walls in a recording of impressions. Ghostly sounding impressions echo back through human evanescence. The room thirsts for presence. The impressions of thousands of voices clamor for individual attention... Voices, laughing, voices whispering, voices singing, voices arguing, voices crying, voices hollering, voices screaming. All of these voices speaking at once — noise. We block out noise. So much noise to block out in our industrial, commercial, high-tech world that we tune out meaningful reverberations. If you concentrate you can hear each sound, individually, at once. Impossible? Detach... Process... Awaken. The nightmare.

I, the needle of recorded impressions, am sensitive to all that is around me. A rock can tell me not to go past the blades of grass because of danger. A tree can tell me stories of its life, the feeling of an omen. Something told you not to go there. Every piece of energy that passes creates an impression in the space around it. The Beast makes us self-absorbed, selfish. We selectively remember moments, people, places and things, but fail to recognize that everything around us is an impression on our existence, and we on it. Reflection. We recall an imprint and replay impressions for others. Story telling is humanity's great gift, but a gift we misuse. We are each a needle to play the recorded impressions of space but the Beast is so noisy we deafen our ears, dulling the roar of distraction. Only a few can hear the natural impressions and to those the old theater is alive. I listen; forcefully tuning out conversations older than myself. Ghosts. Finally... I hear what I'm listening for. A sound amplifies over the others. Through the distortion her voice begins to override and distinguish itself. All I can hear is her now. A beautiful hypnotic tone. She stands prominently on the expansive stage. A spotlight cast upon her. No one is in the audience, no one else exists on stage, just her.

Her illumination dominates the room. Her image radiates. I knew she'd be here. It's 3:00 AM and she's adorned in full costume. I have watched her rehearse before. She hadn't noticed me previously, but tonight she would.

I approach the stage. The sight of this magnificent woman in full 16th century French courtesan dress, reciting lines to an imaginary co-star for an imaginary audience at three o'clock in the morning sends chills down my spine. She catches sight of me but continues her lines; she is a true performer. I pass the front row and stand at the edge of the stage. Her lines speak to me, captivating me in the hypnotic flow of language.

"I only serve one master. I will work for you but I will not serve you. I understand your desire... It is not my wish to do so. Life is not a matter of choice. Everyone has to do things they wish they did not have to do. This for me is one of those things. You are not my true master."

She looks directly into my eyes.

"Hello Professor.... What brings you here?"

She stares at my presence, but looks straight through me. Not having seen this beautiful woman in weeks, my breath loses pace with my heart.

"Are you okay, Professor? Would you like something?"

Many answers to her question flood my mind. I want so much to tell her to touch me. Not an erotic, filthy touch... Any touch at all. A slap. A scratch. Anything would do. My Mistress. She comes to the edge of the stage.

"Professor.... Did you miss me? You know this setting is inappropriate for us. I'm either your student or your Mistress. Which one do you want me to be today? ...I wonder? I think... I think you aren't sure which one you want me to be. Am I right Professor?"

She lifts her dress a little, I can't help but look. She knows what she's doing. I look without remorse.

"Oh, Professor, you want me to be both. It's three in the morning. Is this why you came here?"

Finally I find my voice.

"I came here to talk to you about the class."

"What about the class, Professor? The class is over. I take finals this week in my other studies. Ms. Amen informed us we would not be taking a written test. Only a question which would be deliver to us personally. I'm still waiting on my question. Is this it Professor? Have you come here to ask me something?"

She paces the stage with purpose in each step, lifting her dress little by little as she moves. I count her steps, my eyes travel up her legs to underneath her dress. Flawless. She doesn't walk more than five steps before turning back and walking six. She is positioning me. From my hypnotic state I regain control.

"Your eyes look beautiful in that costume."

She laughs.

"Professor.... You weren't looking at my eyes, do you like what you were really looking at?"

She stops walking. I want to say yes.

"Ms. Emch... I do have a question for you."

Lifting her dress she crouches, further exposing herself. I fight to keep my eyes from between her beautiful legs. She isn't wearing panties. I whisper up to her, standing on the tips of my toes, her beauty almost in my reach. I picture my lips on her as I say,

"Is evil... Freedom?"

Her eyes ignite. She looks out into the theater. Someone is now watching us but I can't take my eyes away from this dream. Looking past me, she smiles and stands tall.

"Professor, your question seems out of place. I'm puzzled. Why would you come here and ask me about evil? You know I don't believe in evil."

Still in her performance... The whispering impressions from the energy in the room begin to come alive.

"Ms. Emch, just because you don't believe in something doesn't mean it doesn't exist. Are you not able to answer the question? Are

162

you conflicted about something? Or are you using your dominance to mask insecurity? What is it about you and evil?"

Her eyes turn from the audience to fix on me. A blazing heat pulses through the room. I expect furious words, a loud response. She lowers to expose herself again. I am aroused. The fuse lit with my question burns through her eyes into my spirit. I refocus from her face to my pleasure. Conflicted – my eyes dart back and forth from her penetrating eyes to the sweetness between her legs. I brace for the explosion ignited by my question.

"How dare you question me. My dominance is not a mask! My dominance is reserved for those who submit to me. You question me about evil knowing you're the reason for your wife's misfortune? The pain I inflicted on you is only a fraction of the agony you put her through. You dare to cleanse yourself through pain and ask *me* about a mask? You believe in good intentions? The mask of Eshu, the sacrificial mask used by the ancients to pay homage to the Gods. Is that the mask you wear? Is that the mask of evil, or good intentions? You ask me a question I can answer logically or emotionally, but I wonder how you would answer your own question, Professor? Can you answer it? Give Me your answer and I will give you what you came for."

Inserting hot needles in my mind disrupt my thoughts. She stands. Assuming a tall, proud stand with hate filled eyes on me. Her new position limits my visual options; I can no longer look under her dress. Her loathsome eyes on her target, all I can do is look away. The needles in my thoughts burn like fire. I cannot hold onto my perceptions. She said I am the reason for Maria's misfortune. Evil... Is evil freedom?

"Freedom is only evil if it goes against what has been established by the lawgivers. The lawgivers establish what is acceptable for a society. Freedom is the ability to do whatever one wishes to do. That is perfect autonomy. We can have comprehension of what is evil by comparing our social to our individual understandings. Think about the Eshu mask used for ritual sacrifice of human life to the gods. In some cultures, or even most cultures, this custom may seem barbaric, but

163

this is how the ancients viewed a healthy religious practice. Most practices now are dictated by the laws of society's justice. The lawgivers outline acceptable customs and practices; without the lawgivers' consent, those same practices are not allowed by law enforcement. The law dictates society's definition for the standard of evil. So, yes. Evil lies within autonomous freedom."

She lowers herself exposing my obsession, a reward for my answer, she says,

"Evil is freedom... Hmmm... Freedom is evil.... Without lawgivers why is freedom evil, Professor? Is it for the same reason you keep losing your wife?"

I am abruptly pulled from my euphoria. Another needle sears into my thoughts. Stinging, sharp intrusions that disrupt the fantasies of tasting her sweet flesh with the harsh reality of Maria. Is what I went through with my wife the same thing that makes freedom evil?

"Ms. Emch, I didn't say freedom is evil. I said, evil lies within freedom. All liberties don't consist of evil, but all evil does carry an element of freedom. So, I cannot answer your question about my wife, but I can say, what happened to Maria is evil and neither she nor I experienced any freedom."

She stood removing the view of her sweet flesh; her disapproval clearly displayed. I struck a nerve. Challenging her dominance, I rebel.

"It's your turn to answer the question. Is evil freedom?"

She smiles, looking past me into the auditorium. I'm invisible to her. She displays her dominance in full majesty. I am insignificant. I crave her approval. She says,

"Freedom is evil... All freedom is evil, Professor. Freedom, as you say, must be dictated by lawgivers. So how can freedoms outside the lawgivers' definitions be acceptable freedoms of society? The lawgivers tell us what freedoms are acceptable; the individual does not decide what their freedoms are. Any freedoms outside of the lawgivers, is evil. Right? As you said yourself, Professor. How can we have true freedom in society when freedoms must first be agreed upon?"

Arrogant words in a tempting tone. She ignores me through her distant eyes. She looks as if she is about to bow. I am not worthy of her attention. She is a royal princess and I, a lowly subject, basking in my own admiration of her. I pray for her attention like all the rest.

"Professor,"

Still not looking at me.

"Professor... Am I right? Is true freedom evil?"

Squinting her eyes now she looks at me.

"Am I right, or not Professor?"

"No."

She doesn't understand. Before I can speak, she bursts into fury.

"You challenge the belief of the covenant, Professor! *You* are a disrupter of order. Your class is evil and you are evil. We know what you are. We know who you are. How did you think you could hide from us?"

My heart became a canon in my chest. She is one of them. She was in the class. I – I – allowed her to have me at mercy. I gave her my power by craving her touch. She wasn't real. She was fake. The voices come alive all speaking at once while she glares at me.

"You can't hide from us. You can't hide from me. We control the world. You have no control over anything. We are watching you. We will find Carl and the rest of the underground."

"Professor?"

Her voice overrides the others, jolting me back to the present reality. My needle skips lines of the recorded impressions.

"Professor? Are you okay?"

"Yes, Yes, I am fine."

"Can you please explain how my answer is wrong? I need to understand. Is true freedom evil?"

She kept staring out at her audience. I jump onto the stage and still she refuses to look at me. I keep my distance for fear of upsetting her. She stands center stage, the glow of her green dress in the spotlight reflects eerily on the floor. Her eyes were softer. I'd never seen this look before, so vulnerable and tender. That's why she wouldn't face me. The trail of a single tear marked her cheek. She retains her composure. Her grace stands firm and proud in the spotlight. She needs to know the answer. *Is true freedom evil?* I spoke,

"True freedom only exists in the perspective of the individual. What's freedom to one person is not always freedom to another. Take traditional Muslim female dress. To some, Muslim women being able to shed their traditional clothing for some other type of clothing represents a type of freedom."

She looks at me and says, "What does that mean for women of other cultures who don't wear that dress? Are we fools, taking our freedom to dress as we wish for granted? Is this all just a bunch of fantasy conjured up in the collective mind of a society? We all believe we have freedoms, but those freedoms live only in the acceptable established practices of our societies and cultures. What you're saying, Professor, is that true freedom is the fantasy one believes in their mind?"

She struggles with these foreign concepts of Truth. The world she knew to this very moment is now being called into question. Everything she's learned conflicts with what I just said – the Truth – we're all in a fantasy.

"Yes. True freedom is a fantasy. Most are like drones, stimulated by electronic impulses sent through media. Believing what we are shown by the media is only part of what controls us. Laws and education do the rest. With very little time for independent thought, how many people in the world actually have time to think without the inundation of outside impulses and messages? How many people have time to think without the interruption of society's daily obligations? How many people think without the infiltration of troubles or worry caused by the outside influences of civilization? How many people think outside of customs, practices, and traditions in their immediate influences? Our minds are conditioned and trained from birth to believe this is normal. Give me a newborn child and wherever on Earth that child is placed they will be products of that environment, from language and diet to social customs. This is the way of the world. We have no true freedom, only the illusion of freedom. Just like the stage and the performance of actors."

I walk into the spotlight.

She looks softly into my eyes and says, "If true freedom doesn't exist, then why did you ask me the question about true freedom being evil or not? What does evil have to do with it, Professor? Is this an evil fantasy?"

I wrap my arms around her waist. Her warm, soft body presses against me. She feels so good. The first time I've held her. We stand in the spotlight.

"Evil is the foundation this civilization is built upon. It took pure evil to design this. I asked you that question for you to open your understanding to what this is. It is far greater than you can know at this time from one question. As time goes on, you will understand. We are inside of a monster that is our Master."

She whispers, "I know, Professor. I know."

Applause echoes through the theater. A figure stands alone in the vast sea of empty seats. The stage lights shine bright in my eyes, but I can still see the silhouette of a woman standing in the back row; the petite figure clapping. I let go of Ms. Emch and call out,

"Who are you?"

Silence.

"Who is that?"

Nothing.

I jump off of the stage. The small figure moves quickly. I give chase. In my mind I know I will not catch up, but I have to try. Curly locks bounce as the pixie runs to the exit. The lights of the university outside offer enough for me to see her face. It is the woman I've seen with Ms. Emch. The woman I'd seen in class the day I dismissed those who had not been selected. The woman I'd seen slap Ms. Emch during our class in the park. She has been watching. She must have been watching for a reason. I turn back to the stage, my obsession is gone. I am alone listening to the echoes of laughter and applause from the voices in the auditorium.

Chapter XVIII: Speak Your Mind

In search of insight I stagger through the hallway. They look at me as if I belong here. There are no more surprised looks at my disheveled appearance. I don't know how long it has been since I've showered. My shower is in my home. I have no home. They tell me I cannot go back. I sleep wherever it finds me. Here, my natural scent and my natural appearance are less upsetting. I find that soothing as I make my way to his door. Being comfortable in a place that accepts me for who I am gives me peace. I walk in the room.

The smell of mothballs, medicine, and hospital food have become familiar. It even seems to overpower my stench. As usual, he doesn't turn to acknowledge me. The recording begins,

"Been a while, ain't it? I haven't been much for calculations of time. It just comes and goes for me. I think that's why I'm so old."

A pause.

"I don't feel like the second oldest person on Earth. Once I got past 60 it all felt the same. What's a year older? What's a year younger? I know the lady who's older than me probably feels the same way. We've both just been here a long time."

He fell quiet. Staring out of his window, he takes a deep, troubled breath.

"You know what always gets me? Why do people think that natural oil and gas are resources to just be used up without regard? It seems a lil' crazy to me. There's got to be a good reason Earth has so much of the stuff. Natural crude oil is everywhere on the planet, and yet to us it's only a way to power vehicles and homes. What does the planet need the oil for? How long has it been since you bathed properly? Are you okay?"

I want to say something... I think I did say something. Hadn't I? He didn't hear me? Why doesn't he hear me? I don't remember the last time I took a bath.

He continues, "It's okay if you can't remember the last time you bathed. You're in a new place. I get it. You still have three students left to see. You need to focus your efforts here and understand what happened to Maria. Do you believe in destiny, Adam?"

Turning from his window, he looks at me. How does he know my name? How did he know Maria?

"Do you believe in destiny, Adam?"

A string of saliva dangles on his beard like the silk from a spider.

"Destiny. Do you believe?"

My mouth can barely open. I want to scream. It feels like I'm screaming. I haven't spoken a word but I'm saying, *Yes! Yes! Yes! I believe in destiny.* He smiles and turns back to face his window.

"Think about what power, is. Think about what you witnessed. How do you figure you both ended up at the same laboratory where those experiments were taking place? You and her with the perfect DNA to reunite the bloodline: even thirds of the three humans combined to create the 99.9% human mother. You two created the Princess. Do you think that's chance?"

He pauses and turns to look at me again. His words delivered through labored breaths.

"There is no such thing as coincidences; no accidents. The blood is drawn to itself."

He chuckles through a cough, transforming it into a raspy cackle. Gasping for breath, his aging body exhibits more discomfort than joy. Nevertheless, he continues. What does he find so funny?

"You know what's a hoot about this age of human understanding? It's the funniest thing ever."

Wheeling himself toward me I can see the time etched into his face. The man coming toward me has been living and breathing longer than only one other person on Earth. I feel as if I should bow, as though a power from above has struck me, my legs are weak. I buckle to my knees. He wheels up to my face. The smell of medicine on his breath tickles my nose. Without humor in his face or voice he says,

"The funniest thing about us humans is that despite all of our medical, technological, and creative innovations, we don't understand who we are and where we originate."

169

"I can tell you this for certain, all humans are related. We have the same origin. The three different strains of people are brothers and sisters. Some folks hear this and will become upset or argumentative. They just don't want to believe they are related to those they despise. They believe in the imaginary borders that separate countries. Our views on race confuse us – the children of the same mother. The Mongoloid, the Caucasoid, and the Negroid... Humanity. "

Wisdom. I feel the subconscious, instinctual doors unlocking in my thinking. I can almost see my daughter. With great effort and obvious discomfort, he leans in closer.

"You want to know how different groups of humans have the same mother? It's because of environmental mutations. Just living in and feeding on different parts of the planet."

He cackles, easing back into his chair, exchanging amusement for breath. Mutation?

"Yes. Mutation."

How does he know what I'm thinking?

"I know what everyone is thinking. I've been here longer than all of you, except one. It isn't destiny that brought you and Maria together. It's not destiny; it is design. This has all been done by design. You are here and it's no coincidence that you selected me for your class. Were you influenced? Think about it. How did I come to you? Did you find these profiles yourself or were they given to you? Did you find Maria or was she brought to you? The greatest trick the devil performed on the world was making the world think he didn't exist. Choices that have been given to you are not under your control. If I give you five cards and tell you to pick the one which most relates to you, how do I know what card you're going to choose?"

My life does not belong to me.

"Answer the question. How do I know what card you're going to pick? Answer!"

His question takes me too far into thoughts I do not want to have. I know how he would know. All of the cards are preselected before I see them. Before presenting them, he already knows my preferences. The other four cards predetermined as ones I will reject. There is no

170

way I won't select my favorite card, the one he wants me to select. That is what he means by design. The way they control humanity. They design our options and give us the illusion of choice. In our delusion, we believe we have a choice.

"Yes, now you understand how you and Maria came to be together. Bringing the components together to recreate the original Mother is like having a child with every human on Earth inside one body. They have been tracking and tracing this bloodline for centuries. You know what they want and you know how important it is for them to have her. A seemingly unimportant individual wouldn't understand why, but you know -- you know it's true."

How? How can I be so important as to contain the direction of human life in my DNA? I'm just an ordinary man.

"No human is ordinary. We are the highest form of existence on Earth. Yeah...Yeah, some tree huggers, marine people, and animal people may beg to differ but... it is true. Human existence on Earth is the only existence where infinite imaginations and realities are able to come alive. Our minds have the ability to conjure creations and inventions that don't exist naturally. Our societies consist of make believe social contracts of man's law, all created from imagination and only because we believe are they able to become reality. That's all from imagination. How is this not a higher form of existence? The ability to create your dreams and make them real. Look into an untouched forest, desert, a vast ocean, or a low valley and tell me how we pulled cars, airplanes, and computers from it? How do we come to be in a world that doesn't naturally produce the things we use every day? Light at night? A spectacular feat. We control and create fire. How can anyone say this is not the highest form of existence next to being God? We create whatever we want in this world of appearances. Human dreams come into physical form."

He pauses, giving me time to absorb his words.

"Money is make believe! Yet look at its control on reality. You see, the more we believe in something, the more powerful that something turns out to be. A small group of indigenous Australians living in a part of the country that has remained undeveloped since the Earth's creation. The area was believed by big oil companies to contain vast amounts of natural oil and gas. The only thing standing in the oil companies' way from drilling was the native tribe; a tribe of people who have been on that land more than 5,000 years. The oil company offered them a billion dollar partnership... *a billion dollars...* That's one thousand millions. Give a thousand people a million dollars; give one million people a thousand dollars each. The nature of some is not the nature of all. A thousand dollars can still mean a lot to a person in this day and age. Some may take it for granted, but it can grant a few wishes here and there. My Ma used to say, *Money grants people's wishes.* You can tell a lot about a person's thoughts by how they spend their currency. This is that person's wish and every wish comes at a price. Remember now, someone's got to sell the wish in order for you to buy it and people have been known to commit any act to have a wish granted."

He smiles.

"Most folks don't understand... beliefs control their lives. That village didn't take the money. They told the executives of that oil company that they would rather live under the fury of God's wrath than to watch them drain the blood of the Earth. I want to go to that village. I heard that story on the news and I'm not always sure about everything I see on the news. That village might not even exist, but if it does I'm going to find my way there. I wouldn't mind being laid to rest in a place like that. A place on Earth that has not been consumed by this Beast we call society. It sounds like a dream."

He squints his eyes, closes them, and winces. He groans, then clears his throat.

"We are surrounded by the blood of Earth!"

The pitch of his voice is noticeable higher.

"Plastics and synthetics, we suck the blood of Earth like mosquitoes. Look at the oil wells pumping and sucking. Look at them! Our flesh and bones dissolve into the Earths heart through its veins and arteries."

He looks at my shoes and slowly makes his way up to my chest. His vision locks on my upper torso. I look down to see what he is

172

staring at. Is there something wrong with my shirt? I see nothing. There isn't anything there. I look to him with question. He is no longer looking at my chest. My eyes are met with a fierce stare. What had he seen on my chest?

"Whenever they try to drill deep into the earth, pressure forces them out. Earth is fighting to protect its heart. Would you want some curious insect drilling aimlessly into your body? We don't feel Earth as a single life. It's so magnificent that we break it down into atmosphere, land, and water. We don't see it as a complete organism. That is like separating you into individual parts and assigning those individual parts life independent of the others. That don't make sense, huh? That's how most schools want you to look at Earth. That's the reason we're taught this beautiful organism holds no feelings about the way we treat it. If we knew the truth about how Earth feels, we might stop what we are doing... Sucking, hurting, destroying for our own needs. When they discovered we could bring more dreams to life using the blood of Earth, the planet's feelings and emotions went out the window. Instead of loving Earth's treasures, we dig and suck like blood thirsty, flesh mining parasites. These plastic synthetics derived from oil are a major part of everything around us. Dreams and inventions made possible by synthetic materials. You know what cancer is? US! Something alien interfering with your nature."

His eyes unlock from mine and dart frantically around the room. Sweat is pouring down his head. I look around at all of the objects that contain some type of plastic: pens, the television, the food tray, cups, the frame around The Last Supper. Our synthetic cancers are extracted from nature's pain; it's evil to hurt the very thing which sustains you.

"People are controlled by the few, not the many. Most of us humans are only concerned with the illusions presented to us. The carefully selected choices presented to us to blind us to the true nature of reality. Does it make any sense to live in a place you destroy? I'm not a tree hugging hippie. I'm just a man who's lived a very long time. I have come to understand what I am as a human being. We can create and give birth to our imagination and this magnificent planet helps and allows us to do so."

He turns and wheels back to his window. A peaceful energy seems to guide him in this process.

"I wonder what treasures we'd have if we were good stewards of this planet we call home? I wonder what we'd do if we knew what we really... I'm... not sure if I can establish who They are... How They, you, don't even know who we are. Who I am? Who you are? How do you know who I am? How do you know who you are?"

Slowly he wheels back toward me. His shoulders struggle as he heaves his arms forward moving the wheels of the chair. I'm thinking, *Why,* as I stare at a man clearly in his final years of life, *Why, doesn't he have a motorized wheelchair?* He inches closer to where I sit on the floor, *Why?* He could've easily gotten a motorized chair and it would have surely eased his mobility. At the twist of a small joystick or touchpad, his chair could move with ease. A man in his condition should have more comfort. Wow... I get it. I understand. Comforts make you weak. Then you form attachments to things you can't live without. Out of breath and in extreme discomfort, he stops in front of me. His odor of medication and decomposition excites my nostrils.

"How do you know who I am when you don't even know who or what you are?"

Each word is a struggle.

"Imagine if you found out you were something other than what you have been taught? Think about it. Who told you how we came to be? If you are spiritual, who taught you how to practice your faith? Without blind faith, none of this can easily be explained."

He coughs and leans in closer, the stench of death invading my senses.

"You have no idea what we are. They lied to you. They lied to me. They lied to all of us. We are not what we have been taught."

A distant look comes over his face. So many times he's avoided my eyes and today I have lost count of our face to face encounters. He begins wheeling away from me. He still struggles, but this time he seems not to be in pain. He doesn't wince or grimace, he doesn't show any effects of strain. He wheels himself away with purpose, a man on a mission. I know where he is going. I knew what was happening. I've seen this before. Mumbling under his breath. I am not sure what he is saying, but it sounds like he is talking to someone. The closer he gets to his window, the faster he whispers. I wish I could understand what he is saying. At window he sighs having reached his sanctuary, a place of comfort and ease. He closes his eyes for a brief moment and inhales deeply, peacefully.

"My brother Vern, asked me one night when we were kids what would happen if all the people who knew how to run the world disappeared and all that was left were people who didn't know anything about law, medicine, science, business, or politics. What would happen to the world?"

A faint smile graces his face he says, "The world might be harsh under natural law, but it would make a lot more sense than it does now. You know what I told my brother? I told him... The human race... The human race would start over. We need to start over. It's time. You know where you have to go. ...Please."

He forces another labored breath, his hands grasp the armrests of his wheelchair.

"Go."

He says mid-gasp. His frail body jerks. His hands grip and release. His muscles tighten in convulsion. His eyes burst wide open giving him his favorite view as his last. Then, with no more troubled breath, no more struggled movements, it's over. His head falls back in the chair and he is gone.

Our last session and I hadn't spoken a word. Now, only one word comes to mind. One word emanates weakly from my emotionally exhausted body.

"Nurse..."

I barely heard it myself.

"Nurse!"

My voice cracked.

Draining all that I had left in me, "NURSE!"

175

Chapter XIX: The Truth Revealed: Willows Park / Cemetery

Imagine having the power to move millions of people's emotions and spirits in one second. Imagine having the power to move an entire nation, the power to move multiple nations in a single second. You laugh? There are those who have the power to move nations, control armies, economies, science, technology, and media. How must it feel to have all of that power? Do they still feel human? Alien. There are those in this world who can move most of our fellow citizens' emotions and command them to follow laws within moments. In the time it takes your heart to beat once, the world can change; this is the power those people possess. What it must feel like to be a being above the laws which control human beings? Can you imagine what it feels like to do whatever you want without concern of being held responsible for your actions? Alien! Good and evil doesn't matter, only your desires. Kings, queens, emperors, dictators, and other leaders of nations have lived this way for thousands of years that we know of. Is it possible a completely different group of humans existed on earth before our civilization? We trace our existence back to that which we can find and that is told to us. Some of those who have control countries have called themselves Gods; a feeling that can't be completely human, can it? Alien.

I enjoy our class together. This is a really great time in my life because I have you. A cosmic feeling. I think about our time together now and I see the future. I think of our past time together and it makes our present moment stronger. You are my forever moment. As long as there have been stars in the cosmos, our love has existed; as long as there are stars in the galaxies, our love shall shine throughout the universe. The winds of earth have blown about for billions upon billions of years. Our love has existed since the first essence of creation. An essence hard for mankind to understand. I feel my everything is with you. It's just like you said, our love is a mirror, a reflection of the other. The forces of nature have brought us together. We've been around each other at different points all of our lives and yet it takes us more than 20 years to finally meet. Our parents went to high school together, but barely knew each other. We lived only 10 blocks from one another but never played together. We went to the same schools but because of our age difference, we didn't have the same friends. Now here we are years later, inseparable. This overwhelming attraction I have to you is directed by something greater than desire. Look at all of the forces it took to bring us together. If one thing went a different way, you wouldn't exist in this form in this time and this place. Our maternal grandparents, or our paternal grandparents — what if any one of them was replaced by a different person? What if that person could not have children? Who would we be now? Think about all of the generations it took to make each of us, my love. Science says we would be different people. Socially we can wonder. If one thing went wrong where would we be?

The day I met you, my life changed. Before that day nothing really made sense to me. After that day, my entire existence made sense. We talked through the night and into the early hours of the morning. I knew from our instant connection, our love was meant to be but when I saw the picture of you and your parents in the mall during Christmas, I knew this was something big. My parents rolled me in a stroller into the background of that picture you and your parents were taking. How is that for perfect timing? We have always been around each other and now we are together. I can't wait to see what we do each day and every night…. I can't wait to look back and see forever. In our embrace I feel eternity around us. It is infinite, my love, every moment, since the dawn of creation, has constructed this moment. All of the past moments to create our lives has always been and will always be… our love.

Always my love,

Maria

I read these words, many no longer legible, from a tattered, tear stained letter more as an affirmation than reminiscing. I have read them a thousand times or more. Countless tears, years of unfolding and refolding, and the few times I balled it up in my clenched fist from pain and frustration, an act always followed by obsessive restoration, leaves me with this well-worn letter. My only piece of Maria. I carried it with me the day I left. My hope of forever in this letter more powerful than my actions. My wish coming true could have stopped all of this from happening, I guess, because of my beliefs. Whatever the case, I ran holding this letter as my wish. A wish that all of this is not true and that the forever promised by my beloved Maria would be realized. I never thought for one moment my wish couldn't come true. Even as I hid amongst society's castaways, I never believed that this wish couldn't come true. I didn't think for one second I couldn't have it.

My forever is not in the glorious, blissful love I imagined. My forever stretched before me in a torturous nightmare of pain, loss, regret, and emptiness. Her forever lay in the same knot of pain and misery. Should we have never met? Maybe we were blips on the radar that shouldn't have been. Maybe this moment was one that should have never existed. Was this the *what if* scenario she'd spoken of in the letter? Was this the time and place where a person who shouldn't have been injected, existed? Me? The error in the perfect formula of nature. My life, her life, were they meant to be? One final time I ball up this letter. I close my eyes and I wish this letter had never been written. With all my strength I throw it into the wind. As it leaves my hand it feels like it had never happened. Placing my hands over my eyes I kneel on the grass of Maria's grave. The soft, luscious grass peeks between my fingers. On all four limbs I scream in tortured sobs. The same place I'd held studies with my class, Willows Park Cemetery, my wife's forever. So badly I want to join her, but my fears hold my actions to a wish. Our last kiss filled with every emotion known to humanity. No words necessary. Even with a new face, new identity, and no hint of admission from myself, she knew my eyes. The letter I had read in a drunken daze so many times was more than what we had. I believed my wish had come true. I held and kissed my love. I thought… The forces of a wish brought her back to me. In the deepest crazed, drug-induced state, she knew me.

"That's because we told her you would be there."

A familiar voice. Carl and Ms. Amen draw closer. The wind and a few spinning leaves blow around them. I am ashamed crawling on my hands and knees. His hand on her shoulder, she guides them closer until they stand over me, then with the next breeze she disappears leaving the two of us alone.

"I always know where you are, Adam. I've been watching over you since you were a small boy. Please... stand up. It is time for you to rise from this grave."

My legs fight exhaustion. I'm weak. No sleep since Bug's passing. Carl extends his hand. I place my hand in his. He pulls me to my feet. Ms. Amen returns with the letter I'd thrown to the wind. She folds it back into a perfect rectangle and presses it into my hand. A charge surges through me emanating from the spot the letter touches me; I feel it in my bones. A chill in the warm sun makes the hair on my body stand on end. Again, my wish has come back to me.

"Don't you recognize me, Adam? I've been watching over you most of your life. This is the Truth: We live amongst the stars. Without them, the universe freezes and preserves life in suspended animation. Absolute-zero. The moment the universe creates a star, a once frozen energy comes to life and a solar wind is born.

"This planet is a host for our alien species; a species born to jump from one planet to the next. The creatures of water take it everywhere they go creating the perfect conditions for our life to evolve using a combination of host planets and oceans. To introduce our seas to a new planet, the water must be delivered through a nimbus cloud that rains for a millennium. We, the shepherds of water's planetary transition, hold a dual purpose when the oceans' evolutionary cycle on a host planet is nearly complete. Those who begin the process of life on the new planet live in outer space as outcasts from the previous host planet. They offer gifts of guidance to our evolving brothers and sisters living on the new, resource-rich host planet. This is our evolutionary purpose.

"A thousand years of rains, hurricanes, and lightning energize the activity of life on the emerging host planet. Our oceans fight to travel to the core of the planet through its volcanoes. The millennia of rains from the massive nimbus clouds flood the volcanoes until finally our water penetrates the lava and travels to the core of the planet. When the first drops of water reach the core, the planet is fertilized with waters roaming the valley floors; it is the most beautiful reaction. Upon fertilization, the depleted clouds recede allowing the rays of the maturing star to shine on the land. The vaporous, swampy planet is primed for evolution.

"Our cousins, those traveling through space as castaways following the demise of the previous host planet, can't live a planetary life without physical assistance. After thousands of years without daily exposure to sunlight or gravity, they can only visit. Having evolved to exist without gravity makes some planets dangerous for their alien existence; any pressure other than zero gravity will crush their alien bodies. As our stewards they watch, waiting for us to be born.

"Humans appear towards the end of the planet's ocean life cycle. We only get to enjoy the oceans' final fifteen-million years. That's the time it takes to reach the highest level of evolution as planetary humans. After a million generations, the human species becomes fully alien and goes in search of the next host planet to hold our water. The human species can create anything it dreams. We pass our highly organized structures of cooperative and evolving thought from generation to generation. Each generation becomes more aware and possesses more creation than the preceding generation. Most of who will never know their true purpose.

"Two water planets cannot exist at the same time in a solar system. Without a host planet, our cousins cannot survive in space. They will have to find a place to freeze and await the next star's creation. They can never travel further than the water which sustains them, and they can never travel too far from the star. The host planet is full of minerals and metals which our alien cousins use to restock, refuel, and restore. We live an endless journey of exploration, passing down our knowledge of the universe. As the star expands heating the host planet, the seething lava and oil from water's evolutionary waste boils at merciless temperatures.

"The death of a host planet is a violent bubbling of waste of the waters' life: fossil fuels. The host planet returns to the star. The great stars that heat space to bring life, swallow large parts of their own solar systems as they grows hotter. The last planet able to support the lifecycle of water under the final years of the star is always a somber place to exist. Our cousins born on the last previous host planet colonize orbiting moons to live in the open in front of the final planet's colonization. There is no need to hide the truth then. On the last planet we make preparations for our star's demise. An old star is a sad sight to see. Water is no longer blue, it is purple from the sun's ultraviolet radiation, which now dominates the planet's light. Fiery solar flares shoot from the burnt-out black spots, as massive stellar winds make surface dwelling impossible for un-evolved beings. I'd like to tell you what it looks like to see a star at the end of its lifecycle, but we all freeze in the sun's last years. The orbit of the last planet is long. Everything moves more slowly. Our first planet with a new star will always be the last from the previous solar system. The last frozen planet shoots through space in the final act of our mighty star. Then, we await the birth of our next star."

The Truth revealed, a powerful night in my life: the last night of my innocence. On the base I'd seen the alien creature floating next to my superiors at the government lab; they were working on a weapon. After that night I questioned the validity of everything around me. It wasn't a mistake that I'd stumbled upon this information. I thought they were watching me because of what I'd seen, but they were watching me because of what I was supposed to do.

"What about my daughter. What are they doing with her?"

Somberness overtakes his stoic demeanor.

"Adam, we have the original mother. She is very precious to our preservation. The largest Controllers have worked very hard for many thousands of years to recreate the DNA of the original mother. It's the main reason they created a place for all the lost children of the world to stand under one banner, one country, America."

"Why? Why would you help take my daughter away?"

He lowers his head.

"Adam, we are Protectors, only a chosen few will be allowed to leave here. We balance the direction of humanity. We are the extreme opposition of our brother, and yet we both work toward the same cause. You see Adam, how can we protect the secret if we can't secure it? There is no place left for you to go. It doesn't matter, we will always be there. The universe belongs to us.

"Those who choose our side will journey into the universe and continue our mission. The Controllers of earth, will stay and rule the minds of humanity until the planet is no longer able to sustain terrestrial life. By then there won't be much left to mine. The angry planet will boil with lava and burn under ultraviolet light. The delicious treat from our water's life cycle on a planet: carbon dioxide. It will be the dominant gas on the planet after our oceans are gone. Billions of years of dead life in the ground builds great pressure. We are told to mine it and lessen the pressure of the fossils, now our fuels. If we don't drill for it, it will eventually erupt and explode out of the ground."

He motions toward the graves.

"Slow the oil down, Adam. Trust me when I tell you, your daughter is quite safe. When she begins to menstruate, they will come for her. Until then, the family will protect her."

It's over. My love existed only to be taken away; my wife and the daughter I was never allowed to know. Our love, created billions of years before either one of us took a breath. The love of the first two human beings is an eternal apex which only comes into our realization. A person's love is for them to decide. Eternal; there is no creation, only continuation. Maria and I brought the original blood of humanity together; the culmination of humans' mutated division, once again whole. My daughter, her life as powerful and ancient as love itself. My wife and I have been together before. The rebirth of the original mother created by my blood and the blood of my beloved. Maybe we were not in the exact form of being that we are now, but all the elements it took to make our daughter still lie inside us. Our energy and our love is humanity. The force of the energy is destiny; I'd been foolish to resist the power. Fighting it only led me away from the life I've wanted. Maria and I could have enjoyed more years together. I'd run from her and into a world of discomfort and disease. She died in pain from the denial of the love that was supposed to be her destiny.

182

By a power greater than our individual selves, our bodies and minds were drawn to one another. It was supposed to be our destiny. The reason I ache and yearn to be with her: destiny. I forced myself to suffer punishment under my own masochistic direction. For what? I could have... I should have... I would have... been with her. Now, here I stand as the arrogant, ignorant father of mankind who has destroyed his family to satisfy himself. My selfishness has to end. I owe it to her. I owe it to our daughter. I have to submit to my true master... destiny.

I raise my lowly head toward Carl and ask, "What will happen to my daughter when she menstruates? What are they going to do with her?"

He extends his hand, helping me to my feet.

"Close your eyes friend. I want to show you something."

The spring winds circle around my body whistling through my ears. Holding his rough, time-worn hands I close my eyes. I hear the rustling debris around me, the sound and feeling caresses me as it engulfs my body. The feeling lulls me into the air's soothing breeze. I feel as though I could go to sleep. Carl's grasp stabilizes me. It feels as if we are flying through the wind, deep into Heaven. I am finally free of my form.

"The ancient winds of Earth cooled and controlled, are dominated by our fertile water. It can assume solid, liquid, or gaseous states. It neutralizes almost any other chemical compound. It is vital to our existence. It can nourish, destroy, or change anything it touches. An ocean can overtake a planet. Life exists inside of it. You must understand our part. We are the keepers. When humans appear, the host planet is ripe with minerals, elements, resources, and life. We are its shepherds, created to evolve past the host planet's sustainment, becoming alien to its nature, Adam. We have only a few generations left. This is what it feels like to travel through the universe: no pressure from gravity, endless movement in all directions until it seems like you're standing still and everything moves around you, travel at the speed of life. After they harvest enough human embryos and stem cells, she will rule over the next host planet for a hundred-million years. She is our Queen, Adam. It's time. It's time for you to go off and be who they think you are. It's time for you to fly."

He lets go of my hands and I fly free, soaring high, higher, until a force dictates *no more*; I lose control, spiraling under the force of gravity. I am pulled to the ground. Why did he let go? I have one more question. What if we had had a son instead? What would he be? What would happen then?

I hit the earth with a crashing thud. I open my eyes. I didn't die. I am not where I had started with Carl. I am not in the cemetery, I am in my living room and I am not alone.

Chapter XX: The Lock

Noise. Human noise. In the city something is always "on." Silence does not exist. Quiet is possible, but absolute silence is not. The human body creates noise. In completely sound-proof rooms human subjects can hear their own bodies. A low-level, high-pitched ring can be heard along with the beat of the human heart, digestive fluids, and gases within the body. Absolute silence exists in the space outside of all life. The universe with all its vast creation sits in silence.

My living room feels empty, but I am not alone. Bandages around my wrists stained with blood speak to me of fresh wounds. Sensitive flesh stinging beneath the bandages tells me I am not dreaming. Ms. Thick and Mr. LaDay sit with me. This has to be a dream.

"Hello, Professor," she says, condescension dripping from her words.

"How are you doing?" Mr. LaDay asks while writing something down.

I didn't expect them in my living room, but for some reason I am not surprised to see them. It feels like they are supposed to be here. I look down at my bandages and ask,

"What are you two doing here?"

They appear surprised by my question.

"You don't know why we are here, Professor?"

Her question earns a sharp response.

"If I knew why you were both here I wouldn't have asked. Let's try this again. Why are you both here?"

They look at each other with uncertainty. He touches her shoulder and moves cautiously toward me.

I don't understand.

"We are here to talk to you, Professor," he says, "Do you want to talk to us? It's okay if you don't. We get it."

Ms. Thick agrees, "Yes, Professor, if you don't want to talk that's okay with us. We can come back next week."

Next week... Why, why would they come back next week? I did need to speak. *I guess?* This is the end of class and these two need to graduate. My grip on reality struggles to withstand my mind's true focus. I don't know if my talk with Carl was a dream or reality. All I know is that I closed my eyes while holding his hand and when I opened them I found myself sitting here with bandages around my wrists. Maybe this moment... I snap out of my thoughts to look at the two people sitting in front of me, their faces contorted in confusion. I need to say something.

"Do you remember our sessions with Bug?"

Ms. Thick looks at Mr. LaDay.

"Bug? Oh, yes, Mr. Clark. What about him, Professor?" She says.

My frustration grows; her stupidity always annoyed me. So many times I wondered how she found her way into this class. I laugh to myself. I laugh to myself about myself. I'd chosen her to be part of my class. It seems foolish now. Like so many people in this world who question why things are the way they are, I cannot understand the reasoning of my past self. I want to blame someone for my choices, for this frustration I chose willingly.

"After every session we had with Bug I would go back and sit with him. Sometimes we would just sit in silence for hours; the only two words spoken between us were hello and goodbye. During one of these silent encounters, he told me that every person who wishes to go to the next level of conscious thinking can advance, but only by changing the way they think about what they believe.

"Do you get that, Ms. Thick? Do you understand what I'm saying? Do you understand what it means to change the way you think and understand? Do you?"

She looks to Mr. LaDay day for verification, for a master to submit to, a go-to person for confirmation in the midst of the uncertainty of her own thoughts. I speak before she can answer.

"You don't know what I'm saying. You can't know what I'm saying, because Mr. LaDay hasn't given you permission to speak."

He interrupts, "Professor! I don't think you're being fair in not allowing Ms. Darcy to answer your question, and I have reminded you more than once not to call her by that name. We cannot proceed with this therapy until you are willing to participate. We have removed you from the group sessions to allow you a more comfortable space to speak about what you're going through. You have been through a lot Professor, and we are only trying to help you through this. You cannot blame yourself for what killed your wife and daughter. It is not your fault. You were at work lecturing. It was an ordinary day that went tragically, tragically wrong."

I lunged at him.

"LIAR!"

"Professor calm down. Security! Security!"

"LIAR!"

After all I've been through?! Why is he trying to twist my pain? I am going to strangle the life from him. I will not continue to be a victim. Strong arms pull me away. The hands on my shoulders feel familiar. I see Ms. Amen watching from the doorway, a devious smile painted across her face. With a curled her finger she beckons me toward the door as I am carried toward her.

Ms. Darcy, I mean Ms. LaDay, no, Ms. Thick was pressed against the wall, frozen by my outburst. I scream to them,

"Look... Look... Have her tell you."

"Who are you talking about, Professor?"

Ms. Amen smiles and covers her mouth to hide her grin; her eyes dance as though lit by flames. She stands in the doorway, clear as day, and yet they act as though they cannot see her.

They are all lying. This is a trick!

"LIARS!"

They carry me out the door past Ms. Amen and I see them... I see them all in the observation room, which now houses a ping pong table: Carl, Mr. Macpherson, Bug, Ms. Emch, Maria's doctor, they're all in the room. They watch me as I am carried off. Flashes of their faces contort through twisted visions in my mind. Different faces on different bodies. Ms. Emch's face on Mr. LaDay's body, his face on her body. Mr. Macpherson, in a football helmet, runs his head into the wall. His helmet inflicts dent after dent into the wall with each hit. Their rebellion has begun. The revolution. I knew Mr. Macpherson would be the one to rally the rest. I scream,

"Free yourselves! Free yourselves!"

The strong hands toss me into a rubber cell and slam the door behind me. I lay there; alone with my thoughts trying to make sense of what just happened. I am in the same room where the sessions with Maria took place. *Oh my God.* I scream. How did I get from Carl to here in this room? Papers are shoved through the space beneath the door. A voice on the other side tells me I wrote the words on the papers as a reminder of what happened and how I got here. I am scared to touch them. I rock back and forth. For hours I avoid them. Ms. Amen picks them up and gives them to me to read. It is my handwriting, but I didn't write this. I couldn't have.

You were away on business presenting a lecture to the United Nations. World leaders were considering a change in retributive punishment using your subject and mission as a new form of justice for the mentally ill, one that would be in line with the social contract theory. All of this because of your book, The Silent Mind. That moment seemed like your most triumphant. The interruption of your lecture came with great annoyance. A phone call. What could be so urgent as to interrupt your greatest moment? Nothing. You should have rushed to the phone. You finished the lecture to great applause and when you finished you learned your wife and daughter had been killed in an attack by those who opposed our society. A terrorist attacked the American Consulate where your wife and daughter were watching you speak. A bomb exploded and many innocent people were killed.

This is how I got here? What is this?

Ms. Amen takes the papers. She places her fingers to her lips to shush me. The door opens behind her and in walks Mr. LaDay and Ms. Thick. For a moment it looks like Ms. Amen has disappeared, but I see she is still there, still watching. She hides behind their legs on her hands and knees. When our eyes meet she puts her index finger to her lips. Ms. Amen's advice to be quiet does not feel like a caution for a possible slip of my lip about her presence, it seems an allusion to the secret we keep about the Truth. The water. The fertile planet. Aliens mining earth's resources. I wasn't at a lecture when my wife died, and my daughter isn't dead. I am not a professor. My wife and daughter

188

were not killed in an attack by rebel fighters. All of this... It happened because of what I discovered. Now, my students are gone. Maybe they weren't my students. Just as I had my face changed, theirs could have been changed too. It is the way of the Beast. The controllers and law-givers can alter your appearance, even change your sex. The two people in front of me are replacements. I wonder if the others are too. I only caught a glimpse of Mr. Macpherson's face through his helmet; next time I have to get a better look. Ms. Amen shushes me again; now I can't take my eyes off of her. Mr. LaDay and Ms. Thick look around their legs to see what I am looking at. They are acting as if they cannot see her, but she is there and I know they can see her. Ms. Thick looks at me studiously.

"Is everything okay, Professor? Is Ms. Amen in the room?"

It has to be a trap. This tactic is one they use to implement mind control. She wants to make my mind inferior to hers. She wants to make me feel insane. I need to be calm in my response to her. Carefully, I say,

"No... No, Ms. Amen is not in the room."

Lying, I take my eyes from the image I'm not supposed to be seeing; Ms. Thick looks pleased with my response. I look into her satisfied eyes to affirm my statement.

"That's good, Professor. Can you please tell me and Dr. Grimsley what it is you were looking at when we walked into the room?"

I took in a deep huff of air, more mind control tactics. She wants subjugation.

"I wasn't looking at anything, Ms. Darcy. I am just trying to cope with what happened to my life and my family."

I must say the right things to appease her, acknowledging her as Ms. Darcy, not Ms. Thick makes her happy and reassures her controls.

"Do you understand that what happened to your family is not your fault? You are not the reason they died, Professor. The people who did that were not thinking about you or your family. The people who did that were only thinking about their own selfish needs. You have to understand that other people's actions and beliefs are not reflections of you or your truth. Do you understand what I'm saying, Professor?"

189

She wants me to regurgitate the words she's fed me.

"Yes I understand, Ms. Darcy."

I knew a simple agreement wouldn't be enough; my only way out of this maze of indoctrination is more submission. Even if I believe otherwise, my words and actions will have to reflect the things they want me to believe. Overt resistance will only destroy society as well as the individual. Like every good citizen under this social contract, I have to submit to the will of the city or suffer its punishment for disobedience. Mr. LaDay, I mean Dr. Grimsley, smiles. He wants in on the part of this part of the process.

"What exactly do you understand, Professor?"

He doesn't smile outright, but I detect a smirk and the pleasure he feels by eliciting my response. It made me want to lash out at him. He was testing me to see if I would break. He's set it up perfectly, but I am ready for his challenge.

"I understand that no matter what I do I cannot change what has happened to me or my family. People with twisted beliefs brought this pain to my life. Their misguided direction is what plagues our society and I will not rest until everyone knows the truth about what happened. No I... Haven't fully recovered from my loss and I could slip back into a delusional state of mind which is sometimes what I feel frees me from the truth of this reality, but I will prove to you that I am working toward the truth of this situation."

He peers inquisitively into my eyes to see deeper into my response. I don't want to blink for fear he'll reject my answer.

"I'm glad you're coming closer to accepting the reality of this horrible situation. We are only here to help you through this difficult time in your life. Society has labeled you a dangerous man, Professor, and this may be the only way for you to find redemption for what you have done."

His words unsettle me a bit. The woman sees I am not prepared for what he just said, she smiles. He talks,

"Professor, you look as if you don't know what we're talking about?"

"Do you know why you're here, Professor?" She says.

190

I want to say I am here because you don't want me to spread the message about what humans really are, and that our alien evolution is almost complete. I want to say we are all slaves dependent on a master who only seeks to make us more dependent on comforts and luxuries.

"Professor, are you okay?" She inquires.

"Yes, Professor are you okay? You look as if you don't quite understand our question. Do you know how you got here? Do you remember what you did?"

Whispering to him loud enough for me to hear she says,

"Doctor, I don't think he knows what we are talking about."

He looks at me and responds to her like I am not there, like I cannot hear him.

"Yes, it's worse than I thought. He's completely blocked out the event. If it doesn't exist, then it didn't happen. Classic case of disassociation. Until he remembers what happened, he will never come to accept the circumstances. He is rationalizing with a missing piece. Please get the door Ms. Darcy, we may need to prepare a room. I'm going to have to explain to him what happened."

She gets up and goes to the door. Ms. Amen scurries out of her way. She gets behind him and smiles at me, sticking her fingers in her ears. He says,

"Professor, shortly after your wife and daughter were killed you went back to work at the University. Your co-workers said you were distant and kept talking about government oppression and conspiracy theories. You told them you were a scientist hired to teach an experimental class about the true purpose of humanity. You had an outburst at a late night school play in which you jumped on stage screaming at one of your students. Then two days later you walked around the football field with a bow and arrow trying to hit imaginary targets during the track team's practice. The dean felt it was best to put you on a sabbatical from the University. The next day you walked into his office and shot him, claiming he was an alien Protector. You left his office and shot four more students."

The final blow to my sanity.

"What?"

I have nothing left. Even after taking everything they still wanted more. This challenge I cannot meet. I face them with tears in my eyes, wishing he'd spare my worthless life. I'd do anything for him to reverse this affliction. What can I do? They killed my wife, took my daughter, destroyed my friends and replaced them with lies. I break down in tears at the finality of it all. He isn't going to spare me. I have to be something that does not reflect who I am. I look to the bandages on my arms. They aren't even going to let me go through death. He says,

"Professor, we are only trying to help you. We understand that stress made you do what you did, and you are normally a good natured person. Obstacles and conditions can hurt in ways some can't even contemplate. How many can explain the pain of losing everything you love in one day?"

My heart flutters with his insult. It only takes a heartbeat for life to change. Ms. Amen waved goodbye. The door opens and two large orderlies stand in the doorway. Ms. Darcy defines the futility of my struggle.

"My heart goes out to you, Professor. I know you aren't the monster they made you out to be in the news reports. You are a brilliant man who should be able to help others in this world to be better people. Your actions brought you here today, but this is no one's fault. Even the officer that found you said he had never seen a man in more pain and agony. He said you clung to your wife's headstone so tight that your fingernails etched marks in the stone. We know you loved her, Professor. We will help you get closer to the closure that you need."

The orderlies advance toward me. The weight of the doctors' words had emotionally drained me. I can't move. Mr. Grimsley, I mean Dr. Grimsley, Mr. LaDay speaks,

"It's time for you to go to your room. We will be back to see you tomorrow after recreation. Please go with the hospital staff. Everything will all make sense someday soon. For now, go and get some rest, Professor. Everything's going to be all right. There's a future for you here."

One of the orderlies reaches under my shoulder and lifts me to my feet. The other grabs under my opposite arm. I am lead down a familiar walk, like déjà vu, until finally we stop in front of a door.

They pause, one asks, "Do you have the key?"

The other pats himself with his free hand,

"Yup, here it is. Doc would have been pissed if we didn't have the key."

I look down at the key. The exact key Carl had given to me. It fit the lock to the door. I know what to do. I walk inside.

"You be good, Professor," one of them says.

"Your medication and dinner will be here soon."

The door closes and I am left to absorb what I just experienced. *The Truth.* I fall to the ground, sobbing into my hands. The choices I made to do what I believed put me here. I didn't construct the walls which confined me, but I might as well have cemented every stone. A chill reaches deep into my bones. The sound of brush rustling in the wind. I look up at the door and there stands Ms. Amen. I screamed until the strength in my voice gave out, and still I persisted in a hoarse pitch until the only thing left for me was hyperventilation. Gasping, I look to the door that opens to this reality; Mrs. Amen smiles holding a radio in her hand. She waves then presses play and the voices of our recorded sessions echo in the quiet place.

Chapter XXI: Medication

"Medication... Medication..."

The soft voice beckons. It wakes me from my sleep. It's evening; still in the same day of revelation. I might as well take whatever they have to give me. The slot in the door opens and there she stands: the curly-haired woman who'd struck Ms. Emch. The same woman from my class on the first day.

"Hello, Professor. Time for your medication. This will help you sleep so you can be well rested for recreation in the morning."

She stands before me in all her glory. The triumph in her voice emanates clearly through the smile she wears. I don't think I've ever felt a smile before today. The curly-haired woman, my nurse, wears the same uniform as the little nervous one who always interrupted my sessions with Bug. She's been altering my reality, interrupting the perceptions of what I am doing. Even the last time with Ms. Emch in the theater, the curly-haired nurse had been there – shifting the reality of the situation. I never got the chance to say goodbye.

"OK, here we go. Here's your medication. Don't look like that, Professor. It's okay. You can take these pills. They won't hurt you. We aren't going to let anything happen to you. Look at those bandages. I wrapped them myself. Trust me, Professor. Take these pills and you will feel much better, then tomorrow you will go to recreation. You always have fun at recreation. All of your friends are there. There you go... That's right. They won't hurt you."

I look at the little pills. *How bad could it get?* I think. If I die, I'll be free and if I lose my current state of mind, fantasy can defeat this reality. I take the pills. She smiles.

"Good job, Professor. You enjoy your night and I'll be back in the morning."

She closes the slot in the door, turning to walk down the corridor.

"Why are you doing this to me!?" I scream, pounding my fists against the door. "Why don't you just let me die?"

She continues to walk, unfazed as if she doesn't hear me.

"Please... please... stop this... Why are you doing this to me!? Let me die! Just...let me die!"

"Medication... Medication... Medication..."

Her voice grows faint as she continues her course until I can no longer hear it. I'll show them. I'll be ready for her tomorrow. My mood begins to change. Slowly, everything I see blurs into lights at the end of dark tunnels; two lanes in one direction. I feel numb. Ms. Amen fluffs the pillow on my bed; the sheets envelop me in warmth and comfort. I curl into the fetal position and she pulls the covers over me. In this moment life doesn't seem so bad. Sleep.

"Baby... Baby... Get up." I lift my heavy eyelids to see through the dense fog, her face. My beloved Maria. Tears well in my eyes. I'm trembling.

"Maria, baby I had a horrible nightmare. I dreamed about a world without you. Baby, I'm scared."

"Shhh, you will never be without me. Whenever you close your eyes, I will be there."

"What? What do you mean? Is it true what they said happened? Why can't I remember our daughter's name? Am I crazy? I don't know what to believe."

"Shhh... It doesn't matter if it's true or not. The only thing that matters to any human is what they believe."

"Then is it true, baby? Is it true what Carl told me about the water cycle?"

She looks at me with soft, loving eyes.

"Don't worry my love, it will all make sense soon. Your thoughts are important. You can create your dreams and make them appear in the world."

"Can I recreate you and make you real? You are always in my dreams. I want you to be here."

"I am here, baby. I'm always here. I live in your dreams and no one else's. In your world I always exist. I am part of you. Don't let them control your thoughts, baby. You aren't crazy. You're in the middle of a war and the spoils of that war is your existence."

"Medication... Medication... Medication."

The words anger me as they snatch me from my dream. It is her again. The slot opens.

"Good morning, Professor. How did you sleep?"

She smiles. Her evil works are never done. She alters minds with a smile. I hate her smile. My stomach twists in knots, fearing her poisonous touch. Venom drips from her lips,

"Looks like you slept well. I'm going to always make sure you're okay, Professor. I'm just delivering the doctor's orders. Here you go."

More pills. I don't want to touch them.

"Come on, Professor, don't mess up your day. It's a beautiful morning. If you don't take your medication, you can't go to recreation. These are the pills that make you happy. They wake you up too. Come on, here."

She threatens me to make me take the pills, another tactic: *do this, or else.* I need to go to the rec room to find out what all this means. Who else is here? I take the pills.

"Open your mouth, Professor. I have to make sure you swallowed them."

I do as I am told.

"Good. Enjoy your rec time."

She closes the slot in the door and wheels her cart away.

"Medication... Medication... Medication..."

Once again I listen as her voice moves further and further away until her siren's song can no longer be heard.

Hours pass. I find myself pacing the floor. Ms. Amen sits on the bed. I wish she could talk. I wish she could hear me. She just sits there looking around. I begin to laugh uncontrollably. I cannot escape. It doesn't matter what I do. It doesn't matter what I believe. It doesn't matter what really happened. It doesn't matter if what Carl has told me is true or not. There isn't anything I can do. The Professor of Truth. Ms. Amen gets off the bed and walks to the door. She places her hand on the ground. Looks up at me and smiles. The slot in the door opens.

"Professor," the orderly says, "do you want to go to recreation?"

Ms. Amen nods her head in affirmation. The pills are working.

"Yes. Yes. I would like to go to recreation."

"All right. All right. We've got another for single rec."

He leads me by the arm down the cold hospital hallway. We walk in silence until we make it to another door. He opens it.

"This is as far as I go, Professor. All of your friends are inside."

They are here. I hurry into the room. My friends, my students, my class. Before the orderly closed the door I overheard him say another tactic to confuse me,

"I don't understand how a guy can be so happy to spend more time in a room by himself. He really thinks there's someone in there."

The other says, "Yeah, the power of the human mind is amazing."

I stand in the center of the room and laugh, finally surrounded by my friends. Ms. Emch, Bug, Carl, Mr. Macpherson, the Dean, all here. The fight is still on. Bug wheels over to me; I am so happy to see his face. The Protectors are trying to trick me into believing this isn't real.

"Carl," I say, "what do we do now? We have been captured."

The second oldest living human being, my friend, calm and collected says, "We wait! Nothing lasts forever. At least we will all be together. The prisoners of Truth," he laughs, "The starship will come."

"I thought you died, Bug."

He laughs.

"Nobody ever really dies. Come on buddy, let's go look out the window. The ship is coming."

I close my eyes and see Maria. I wish she could see the ship. She can. We have one vision. I open my eyes and all of them are gone. I'm alone. They got on the ship without me. I look out the window. There's nothing there. No class. No ship. Only my screams. The staff comes running in. The curly-haired nurse frowns.

"His medication is wearing off."

[i] "Stephenson (1967) trained adult male and female rhesus monkeys to avoid manipulating an object and then placed individual naïve animals in a cage with a trained individual of the same age and sex and the object in question. In one case, a trained male actually pulled his naïve partner away from the previously punished manipulandum during their period of interaction, whereas the other two trained males exhibited what were described as "threat facial expressions while in a fear posture" when a naïve animal approached the manipulandum. When placed alone in the cage with the novel object, naïve males that had been paired with trained males showed greatly reduced manipulation of the training object in comparison with controls. Unfortunately, training and testing were not carried out using a discrimination procedure so the nature of the transmitted information cannot be determined, but the data are of considerable interest."

Sources:

Stephenson, G. R. (1967). Cultural acquisition of a specific learned response among rhesus monkeys. In: Starek, D., Schneider, R., and Kuhn, H. J. (eds.), Progress in Primatology, Stuttgart: Fischer, pp. 279-288.

About the Author

Tshombe Amen is a talented author with a unique voice and viewpoint. His works are filled with twists and turns, often requiring the reader to pay close attention or risk missing something. His books are masterfully woven together in a fashion that begs readers to reread them to get the full impact of his words.

Tshombe began as a mystery writer, but continues honing his craft as he ventures into new genres while maintaining an air of suspense in all his works. His darker tone is made poignant through his poetic style and structure.

Upcoming Works

Tshombe's next planned release is the second book in his *Fantasy of Love* series. Centered on the strained relationship of a reclusive father and his loving, but resentful daughter, *The Caged Heart* shares a story of love and what we will sacrifice and endure to feel its warmth -- even when all we've known are the chills of love's shadow. The expected release date is mid-2016.

The tentatively titled, *The Serpent and the Dragon*, Tshombe's follow up book to *The Professor* and the second in the World of Appearances series, is sure to spark controversy and creative minds alike with his thought provoking theories that link humanity to both its creation and to its present day politics.

Available Now from TS Amen Publishing
Sarah's Diary
The Fantasy of Love, The Broken Mirror

tsamenpublishing.com

www.ingramcontent.com/pod-product-compliance
Lightning Source LLC
Chambersburg PA
CBHW032007240626
47153CB00003B/1160